PI   ;EVEN
O   RDER

MICHAEL ROBERTSON

Email: subscribers@michaelrobertson.co.uk

Edited by:

Terri King - http://terri-king.wix.com/editing
And
Pauline Nolet - http://www.paulinenolet.com

Cover Design by The Cover Collection

Prophecy: Book Seven of The Shadow Order

Michael Robertson
© 2018 Michael Robertson

Prophecy: Book Seven of The Shadow Order is a work of fiction. The characters, incidents, situations, and all dialogue are entirely a product of the author's imagination, or are used fictitiously and are not in any way representative of real people, places or things.

Any resemblance to persons living or dead is entirely coincidental.

All rights reserved

No part of this publication may be reproduced, stored in a retrieval system or transmitted in any form or by any means electronic, mechanical, photocopying, recording or otherwise, without the prior written permission of the author except in the case of brief quotations embodied in critical articles and reviews.

MAILING LIST

If you'd like to be notified of my news, discounts, and new releases,
you can sign up to my spam-free mailing list at
www.michaelroberstson.co.uk

CHAPTER 1

The attention of the room remained on Seb. He stared back at them, shaking from the adrenaline surging through him.

Then the door burst open, and Seb spun around to see SA standing there. She'd only been gone a minute. Her mouth lifted in a half smile, and her eyes widened. *You're okay.*

The image of his love blurred as Seb cried freely. *I am. You did it!*

We *did it.*

SA ran forward, shoving Owsk and Buster aside. She kissed him so hard it hurt, his lips pressing against his teeth. Not that he cared.

Seb breathed her in, everything else vanishing around him. When they pulled away from one another, he held onto her hands. "I've missed that."

The others waited, giving them their moment.

When they broke apart, Moses walked over to Seb and hugged him. Although he brought his usual smell of fish, and his rough leathery skin scraped against Seb's face, the large shark emitted an uncharacteristic warmth. Strangely paternal, Seb squirmed because of its tenderness.

Moses pulled away, and Seb's attention went to the glazing of his onyx eyes. The deep bass boom of his voice took on the slightest distortion as if his words caught in his throat. "I'm so glad ..." He stopped to cough. "I'm so glad you're okay, son."

While this happened, Seb couldn't help noticing Sparks tapping away on her computer—the consummate professional. Always working, she waited for Moses to finish before she projected an image onto the conference room's wall where Enigma had just been. "Seb might be okay—and that matters—but look at everywhere else."

The footage showed several major spaceports, including Aloo. Chaos already ran through them. Blasters were being fired, swords wielded, and blood spilled.

Seb shook to watch it, his energy at rock bottom. "This is all our fault. The second we kidnapped that slaver, we sent a flare up for Enigma to see. If we'd have gotten out quietly, we would have had time to track them down without them knowing."

While holding his hands in front of his chest, the tips of his long fingers pressed together, Mr. H shook his head. "Not necessarily. We were expecting something to happen soon. The slaver going missing might have forced their hand, but we believe an attack was imminent anyway. We've been trying to find Enigma for years and haven't managed it. Maybe this is the way we need to do it. And you know what? If we have forced them to play their cards earlier than they would have liked, that might give us an advantage too. They might not be fully prepared. Besides, I'm sure your hostage will be able to help us in some way, and the information we have on the slaves gives us a good starting point. We know what's happening out there isn't to do with the *beings* committing crimes; it's much more about the programming they've gone through. We know we need to go after the puppet master rather than getting dragged into a battle on the ground. They're victims in this like anyone else. They're the noise to distract us. The intelligence you've gathered might just be the thing that saves the galaxy."

"Whatever happens," Seb said as he continued to watch the chaos, "we need to act now." As he looked at the rest of his crew, he saw determination in all of their faces. "You all with me?"

"What about your rest?" Buster said.

"I'll rest when I'm dead."

A lifted eyebrow, the reptile's voice dropped. "That might come sooner than you plan."

Buster's stark honesty forced Seb to face what he'd been trying to avoid. A buzz of exhaustion shuddered through him. So he could remain upright, he rested both hands on the back of a nearby chair and pulled deep breaths into his tightening lungs. Could he really do this? He almost laughed at himself. Like he had a choice! After a glance at SA, he straightened his posture. If he had her beside him, he could do anything.

With an impatient flick of his tail, Buster looked around the room before his dead gaze returned to Seb. "So, what's the call?"

The footage didn't play out as a projected image on the wall anymore, but Seb could still see Sparks staring down at her tablet. She swiped two fingers against the screen to flick through different scenes on different planets as she watched chaos erupt around the galaxy. Not close enough for him to get a clear sight of what she watched, it still gave him enough of a feel for what was happening out there. They were lucky to be in the Shadow Order's base, protected by the water surrounding it. He looked at the others for ideas. Then he saw SA and pointed at her. "Your nose."

SA pushed the back of her hand to her top lip. When she pulled it away, some of the blood that ran from it had been stamped on her skin. She looked up at Seb, a paler yellow than before. Always hard to tell because she never moved her mouth, but it looked like she wanted to say something. Then the calm bioluminescence of her gaze snapped back, showing just the whites of her eyes. A moment later her legs folded beneath her and she went down.

Even with his world in slow motion, Seb didn't react quickly enough. He lunged for her as she fell and smashed her head against the back of one of the chairs in the room with a loud *whack!*

CHAPTER 2

The spray from the water lit up cold pinpricks against Seb's face, his eyes stinging from the salty onslaught as he scowled in the direction they were heading. Aloo's spaceport lay on the horizon. Still unable to see much of the chaos, the large clouds of smoke rising up in several spots told him enough. Within minutes of Enigma's transmission, the comms between the Shadow Order's base and the spaceport had been cut off. The fires must have had something to do with it.

Owsk acted as skipper, with Buster beside him. Old friends, the two of them had been inseparable since they'd rescued Buster from his underwater captors. Sparks and Bruke had also boarded the vessel with Seb and SA. Bruke looked around at the other boats in their fleet, and Seb recognised his own anxiety in his friend's crushed features. Sparks glanced from her computer to the spaceport and back to her computer. They were travelling fast enough for the wind to send her black bob of fine hair streaming out behind her. None of them spoke.

Despite the saline onslaught both burning Seb's eyes and

leaving the taste of salt on his tongue, he continued to face it as he watched the horizon, their boat rising and falling with the undulating sea. He had wanted to travel to the spaceport from the Shadow Order's base by air, but he'd been outvoted. He understood why.

As if to highlight their correct decision, Seb watched a small freighter take off in an attempt to leave Aloo. The sky had seemed relatively quiet until the vessel rose up into it. Suddenly a multicoloured show of pyrotechnics exploded from the ground. A fireball engulfed the freighter, smoke lifting into the air while the husk of the vessel fell. A large splash punctuated the failure of the ship's bid for freedom, Seb's stomach sinking almost as fast as the wrecked shell had.

SA must have sensed his anxiety because she squeezed his hand harder than before. When he looked at her, she smiled. The colour had returned to her skin since she'd fainted, and she insisted she felt fine. Although he had to take what she said at face value, he still kept an eye on her.

If they'd heard Enigma's broadcast in the Shadow Order's base, they had to assume every device that could receive the message on Aloo had also heard, and the trigger had found the ears of all the slaves who needed to hear it. And if the footage on Sparks' computer gave them anything to go by, it looked like the same thing had happened on many other planets.

At least eighty percent of the personnel in the Shadow Order's base had taken to boats like the one Seb currently rode in. As he looked to both sides, he saw many tight jaws and many pale faces. Nearly every one of them stared ahead at the burning mess on the horizon. Occasionally, one of the Shadow Order soldiers would look across at him as if for guidance. They were the lead ship. The chosen one had to be the first into battle and had to show them what needed to be done.

The boats moved over the sea, rising and falling with the waves, unrelenting in their forward progress. When they hit the next wave, their ship took off. Seb's stomach lurched with the vessel, and he squeezed SA's hand maybe a little too hard.

Although she winced, she looked at him and smiled. She understood. After all, she'd seen him trying to swim.

Another wipe of his face to clear the saline mist, Seb said to her, "Are you sure you're up for this?"

Both Sparks and Bruke looked over at them. It took their attention to make Seb realise just how condescending he'd sounded. Before he had a chance to reword it, SA called him out. And from the way Buster and Owsk flinched, she'd obviously said it so the others heard too. *I'm fine. Like I've already told you. It was a funny turn, nothing more. I think you should focus on how you're feeling at the moment rather than put your anxiety on me.* She let go of his hand and turned away from him.

"I'm sorry." Seb reached out to hold her hand again, but she ignored his gesture. "You're right, I hate being above so much water. But I do care how you're feeling. I want to make sure you're okay. I didn't mean to patronise you."

The usual warmth had left her brilliant glare when she turned it back on him. *What we've been through so far has been tiring for all of us. I passed out; I'm fine now. End of story.*

After nodding at her, Seb looked at the others. They all regarded him through narrowed eyes. Before he could defend himself, a dark silhouette rose from the ground in his peripheral vision. He looked at the spaceport in time to see the thing burst free from the low-lying smoke. A teardrop-shaped missile, it lifted in the sky, its wide arc heading their way.

CHAPTER 3

Although he kept his attention on the large projectile, Seb could sense the others in the boat looking at the missile too.

"What is it?" Bruke said.

Sparks pressed her computer to her ear while staring at Seb. When she pulled it away, she said, "I've just spoken to Moses, and he said he hasn't got a clue. It's nothing to do with Aloo's defences. It must have been launched from one of the ships docked over there. With so many vessels we know nothing about, they could throw anything at us."

The roar of the boat's engine shook through the flimsy vessel, and they got air off the next several waves. They had straight-line speed, but they weren't nimble. The boat didn't have it in it to dodge at the last minute to avoid being sunk. While pulling his sodden hair from his forehead, Seb continued to watch the missile. They were powerless to the attack heading their way.

Seb looked left and right again. At least thirty boats had left the Shadow Order's base. Many of those on board the ships watched the missile, their jaws hanging loose. It continued on its upwards trajectory as if it could block out the sun.

The second Seb had boarded the boat, he'd worked out where the life jacket was. Were it not for the pressure he felt to lead, he would have had it on from the start. But it wouldn't have filled the rookies with confidence to know the chosen one got palpitations when he went too close to a puddle. However, as the missile hit its apex, he reached for the bright orange safety vest. If they wanted something to lose their nerve over, it wouldn't be him wearing a flotation device. Not anymore.

Before Seb could grab the life jacket, something tugged on his fists, stopping him from reaching down. His world flipped into slow motion. As he looked up at the teardrop-shaped projectile and saw the red blinking light on the front of it, his stomach sank. The missile now flew at them with intent. He called to the others, "It's a large magnet!"

The missile travelled down at twice the speed it had gone up at. Its flashing red nose zeroed in on them, flying straight and true. His fists now dragged above his head, Seb looked at the orange vest by his feet. It taunted him, berating him for not being safety conscious from the start.

The magnetic pull tugged harder on Seb's fists. Just before he lifted from the ship, Bruke and SA both grabbed a hold of him, keeping him anchored.

Within a few metres of hitting them, the red blinking light on the missile turned off. The pull on Seb's hands desisted, and he fell backwards with SA and Bruke. All three of them landed in the metal base of the boat with a loud *tonk*. Cold water soaked through the back of his shirt while he lay on his back and watched the missile fall.

Seb sat up in time to see the teardrop crash into the ship next to them. The contact triggered an explosion that sent out a loud *thoom* of a shockwave. It hit him in the face, throwing him to the other side of the boat and giving him tinnitus as his world spun.

The large splash from the explosion rose at least ten metres into the air, creating a thick wall of water that obscured Seb's sight of the boat it hit. His vision swam as if he'd been whacked with a sledgehammer. As he sat up for a second time, the water landed on them, knocking him back again.

The splash cleared to show both ends of the struck ship lift into the air and meet in the middle as the vessel sank. The boat then vanished from Seb's sight as the rising swell from the hungry sea consumed it.

Owsk cut the motor, and Seb watched on as all the others in the boat leaned over the side to pull in the passengers from the wreck. As much as he wanted to help, he looked at how their ship tilted with the crew leaning out of it. His heart beat so fast his head spun. He moved as far over to the other side of the boat as he could to provide a counterweight to their activity. He pulled the life vest towards him and hugged it to his chest.

CHAPTER 4

⚜

A few long minutes passed before there were no more soldiers in the sea next to them. They'd taken on four new passengers, all of them delirious from the shockwave. Many of the other surrounding boats had done the same, and when he looked, Seb couldn't see any more of the ship's crew in the water.

The first creature to come round had white skin and two holes where a nose would be on a human. It had tiny red eyes, blinking as it clearly tried to find its bearings. A rookie, Seb grabbed its shoulder and looked into its dazed stare. Unable to keep his panic from his voice, he said to it, "Are you okay?"

The creature blinked repeatedly, its breaths running through it in short and sharp bursts. The first moment of clarity settled on its face when it looked from the chosen one to the flotation device he clung onto. It didn't reply, instead offering Seb a confused frown. Why couldn't the great Seb Zodo swim? At least, that's what he read into the creature's expression. Maybe he projected his own insecurities onto the being and created a narrative that didn't exist. He looked back at its frown. Maybe not.

Before Seb could defend his actions, one of the other creatures sat up, frantic in how she searched the other ships surrounding them. She took a few seconds before she leaned over the side of the boat to look at the water. "I think we've lost one."

One too many. Seb dropped his life vest and looked at the space where the ship had sunk. It offered no clue as to where the missing soldier had gone.

The engines of all the boats then roared to life. If they had lost one, they couldn't do anything about it; hopefully it had made its way to one of the other ships. Just then, another teardrop silhouette lifted into the sky. "Damn it," Seb said before reaching for the life vest again and slipping it on. So what if the others judged him? He needed to do everything he could to survive. They all did.

CHAPTER 5

The next large metal teardrop seemed to take an age to rise as Seb watched it in slow motion. It lifted up as if surveying the battlefield, playing god in how it decided who to target next.

A tightening in his chest, Seb tried to pull in a deep breath to unwind it. The ocean spray continued to pinprick his face while he adjusted his legs to accommodate the boat's unpredictable movements. Although he watched the missile, he felt the white-skinned creature with the red eyes in his peripheral vision. It stared at him as if looking for some kind of guidance. But what could he do? He tugged on his life vest's straps so it pulled tighter against his body. The creature whimpered.

If he'd had more time, Seb might have tried to reason with the rookie. He didn't choose any of this. He knew no more about what they faced than it did. His fists were a curse from Moses. That was why he couldn't swim. The rookie shouldn't be scared of that.

For a second, the large missile appeared to hover in mid-air as it hit its apex. The sun as its backdrop, the bright glare added to the saltwater sting in Seb's eyes.

Then it fell, Seb's heart dropping with it.

It took a few seconds, but even with the distance currently between them and it, Seb saw the teardrop wasn't heading for them this time. A space where the already sunken ship had been, he looked across at the next one along. The largest in their fleet, he focused on the captain. A red female from a species he'd never seen before, she had flaccid horns framing her pretty face. He waved to get her attention and then called across to her, "The magnetic pull stops at the last minute."

Although the driver looked at him, she clearly didn't hear anything he'd said.

The splash of the water, the roar of engines, even the fighting in Aloo on the horizon ... he had to compete with all of it as he shouted again, this time so loudly stars swam in his vision. "At the last minute, accelerate away from the missile. It's the only way it will miss you."

The driver continued to stare a blank glaze at him. Then she flinched. Her eyes widened and she looked around. Suddenly the missile didn't appear to be her main thought.

Just metres before it landed, Seb got what had happened. SA next to him, she'd spoken to the ship's driver, clearly adding to the chaos already running through her.

The red flashing light on the missile went off. Seb closed his right hand as if gripping an imaginary throttle. He pulled it back to urge the red-skinned captain to get the hell out of there. He called across at her, "Go now!"

No response. If anything, SA trying to help had only made it worse. The captain froze as she waited for ...

The same shockwave *thoom* clapped through the air. It hit Seb and drove the wind from his lungs as it knocked him backwards like the first one had. He stumbled into one of the benches and fell. A white flash ran through his vision when he hit his head on the side of the ship.

Although not unconscious, a throbbing ran through Seb's skull along with another harsh bout of tinnitus. He worked his jaw to get his hearing back. While poking his right index finger into his right ear, he wiggled it as if it would help. When he pulled it out, it had blood on the tip.

Seb staggered to his feet to see those around him doing the same. His balance off from a combination of the rocking boat and the whack to his head, he moved to the side of the ship closest to the recent wreck. A series of waves from the explosion crashed into them, each one threatening to spill into their vessel.

The others came to Seb's side, tilting the boat so hard it dropped the lip of it just inches from the water. But it didn't go under.

The gunmetal grey of the large boat's twisted frame vanished into the depths beneath them. The unconscious crew sank with it. Those on all the surrounding ships dived into the water to rescue their colleagues. SA, Sparks, and Bruke all jumped in with the rookies, who'd only just recovered from their own wreck.

Seb kept a tight grip on the edge of his vessel and watched on. A larger and more populated boat than any other in their fleet, the sea had filled with the Shadow Order members rescuing the unconscious crew.

As Bruke and SA swam back to the boat, Seb saw Sparks treading water and looking down. Too small to help, she looked to be serving as a marker for a sinking soldier.

When Sparks made eye contact with Seb, he looked around for a spare being. Owsk drove their ship, and everyone else had gone in. He drew a breath to call to a neighbouring boat. All of the crew were already in the water.

The gunmetal grey of the large ship might have vanished from sight, but as he narrowed his eyes to focus, Seb saw the crew member beneath Sparks. He saw bright red skin that was dulling as she sank, the dark water closing around her—the ship's captain.

When Seb made eye contact with Bruke, he inhaled to call out to him. But he stopped. Bruke couldn't do anything; he had his own struggle with an unconscious crew member in one of his strong arms. No one else could help the poor pilot without putting their own survivor in danger.

Locked in a battle with his own trembling body, Seb undid his life vest. It took several attempts to free the catch because of his shaking hands. When he got it off, he threw it down on the deck of the boat and picked up a nearby rope. Slow motion gave him time to think. He tried to shut it out. Too much consideration and he'd change his mind.

Once he'd tied the rope around his waist, he then attached it to one of the metal struts beneath the bench next to him. Not allowing himself any more time, he stepped up onto the lip of the boat and dived in.

When he made eye contact with Sparks and saw her wide panic at what he'd done, he changed his focus and looked at the fading red captain below instead. He didn't need to be reminded of the insanity of his decision.

The water damn near freezing when he hit it, Seb's entire body tensed as he sank. He angled himself so he aimed at the red-skinned pilot. Just one chance, he reached out for her.

Although slightly slowed down because of the resistance in the water, Seb hit the captain with a rugby tackle and wrapped his arms around her, dragging her down with him.

They fell fast. A test for Seb's knot and the rope's strength. It snapped taut, pulling the wind from his body in an explosion of bubbles.

Fighting the urge to inhale, Seb looked up. The surface seemed impossibly far away.

It took extra effort to use his hands in the water, but they weren't so heavy he couldn't lift them. With the creature he'd rescued in one arm, he reached up the rope, gripped it, and turned his hand, wrapping it around the outside of it. As he repeated the process, the rope shortened, pulling them back up again. But they weren't making fast enough progress.

The sound of Seb's pulse ran through his skull. The dead weight of the creature from the ship in his arms, his heavy hands fought against his pull to freedom. He gritted his teeth and continued to wind the rope around his grip.

A few metres from the surface, Seb looked up at the bottom of the boat he'd jumped from. He saw Sparks' small legs above him. At least he had an advocate on the surface. Hopefully she'd find someone to help them.

Every pull drained Seb a little more. A metre of water between him and fresh air. Fire ran through his muscles, and his lungs felt like they'd pop, but he had to do this. He had to keep going.

Half a metre to go, Seb's view faded. Then he heard the splash of Bruke's two strong arms plunging into the water. They reached in and grabbed the red-skinned captain.

When he felt sure they had her, Seb let go. He let go of the ship's captain. He let go of his grip on the rope. He let go of hope. He'd saved her. He couldn't save them both.

Dizzy with his need for oxygen, Seb watched Bruke's wavering reflection. It grew dim as he plummeted back into the darker water.

CHAPTER 6

The heavy pressure on Seb's chest registered milliseconds before the hard rush of salty water exited his lungs. He tried to inhale too soon, pulling most of the warm brine back in again. As he flipped over onto his front—taken over by a coughing fit—something drove a hard whack against his back. It felt like he'd been hit with a club, the pain of the contact demanding most of his attention.

Another hot saline rush. The taste of the liquid itself made him retch harder. It burned on the way out and pooled in the metal bottom of the boat.

After clearing out his stomach again, Seb sat up before dragging himself onto the boat's bench. This time, he hung out over the side of the vessel to be sick.

When the vomiting abated, Seb leaned forwards, rested his elbows on his knees, and stared at his feet. The rise and fall of the boat did nothing to help his nausea, so he looked up to keep his bearings. They were much closer to Aloo.

Both his head and stomach settling down, Seb turned to those around him. He met the stares of many anxious beings, more than had been on the boat before. Bruke, SA, Sparks, and Buster were the closest of the lot. Just next to them, he saw the red-skinned captain he'd saved. She pressed her hands together as if to pray to him. The creature with the tiny red eyes and shock-white skin stood next to her. The judgement the creature had previously looked at him with had now gone. It stepped forward before anyone else could speak, dropped down onto one knee, bowed its head, and held up the bright orange life jacket as an offering.

No need for words, Seb simply took the garment and slipped it on, his arms shaking as he tried to get some of his strength back. A brief shared look with SA, he smiled at her, and she returned the warm gesture. *I'm glad you're okay,* she said.

Seb nodded before he stood up to get a better look at where they were heading. He was already exhausted, and they hadn't even started yet. Much closer to land, pyrotechnics still lit the air above the spaceport—more for show than anything because he couldn't see any ships in the sky. Or maybe not show; maybe more a display of the chaos and wanton destruction they were about to walk into. Maybe the enraged beings had no concept of showing off. Maybe they hadn't jeopardised the comms between Aloo and the Shadow Order's base on purpose. Maybe they had nothing else driving them but the need to obliterate everything in their path.

Because they were now a lot closer, Seb saw the smoke came from burning ships. It looked like every one docked in the port now sat ablaze. He saw beings fighting in the walkways. Blasters were fired, punches and kicks thrown. "How the hell are we going to wrestle this place back under control?"

None of the beings replied.

As much to distract himself from what lay ahead than

anything, Seb looked at the fleet riding with them. They seemed in good health. "I'm guessing there were no more missiles?"

Sparks shook her head. "No. Thankfully."

The silence from every other being on the boat with them spoke of what they were about to face. They'd had longer to watch Aloo as they closed in on the port. Seb's lungs ached from nearly drowning, a pain in his wrist from where he'd wrapped the rope around it, and his throat burned with the taste of salt. He focused on his breathing as the boat bobbed up and down with the waves, the cold spray still hitting his face. If he didn't take this time to be still, he couldn't guess when the next opportunity would come. This was his moment of meditation before they stepped into insanity.

CHAPTER 7

A loud crunch shuddered through the ship when they rode the boat up onto the concrete ground where Aloo's spaceport met the water. Several of the rescued beings fell over because of the abrupt halt. As the lead boat, they hit land first. A second later, the others grounded on either side of them. The scraping sounds ran away from them in both directions. The easy part out of the way, they were now about to run head first into hell.

No matter how many times Seb had tried to settle himself with breathing techniques, nothing calmed his ragged pulse. It didn't help to see the white-skinned creature with the small red eyes pull itself to its feet before vomiting several times. The splash-back kicked up against Seb's legs, and the acrid stench hit him a second later. Not even the strong wind could banish the smell. A flare of rage streaked through Seb, but he couldn't be cross with the wretched thing.

Just before they'd landed, Seb had thrown his life jacket down. He now rested on the edge of the metal ship and led the way by vaulting off the boat to dry land. It took a few wobbly steps before he trusted the ground beneath him wouldn't lurch and sway.

As Seb watched his friends follow his lead, he directed them to where he wanted them to go. Before they'd left the base, Buster had identified this spot as the best place to defend—a cluster of warehouses owned by Moses. After Sparks confirmed the buildings to be empty of any rioting creatures, it seemed like the best spot. Four large structures of identical shape and size, they had an alley about three metres wide between each one. On the left side of the first warehouse and the right side of the last one stood strong fences about five metres tall. They shut off any chance their attackers would have of flanking them. It left just three walkways to defend. They could use them to funnel the insanity towards them.

They'd numbered the warehouses as they approached them. Number one on the left, running all the way across to number four. *SA, you and I are going to go to number two and watch a side of it each. Bruke, number one. Sparks and Buster, number three, and Owsk, number four.* None of them acknowledged his orders. They didn't need to; they'd already discussed tactics.

As Seb ran across the stretch of concrete between where they'd landed and the warehouses in front of them, he unslung his machine gun. Loaded with rubber bullets, they'd gone with the intention to overwhelm them without killing them. These creatures were victims; they didn't deserve to die. Just to be sure his weapon still worked after the soaking, he shot the ground as he ran. A burst of three bullets kicked from the gun, bounced off the ground, and rebounded in three different directions, running close to several soldiers. Seb felt some of the soldiers looking at him as if they wanted an explanation. He didn't give it to them. Even if he had clipped one of them, they were rubber bullets, and they'd had all their force taken from them by being shot against the concrete first.

When he got to warehouse number two, Seb leaned his back against the brick wall framing the building's large entrance. He then poked his head out for a clear view down the alley. Flimsy chain-link fences covered the end of each one. Beyond that, he saw the burning ships in the spaceport. There were no crazed beings ... yet.

Bruke held a similar position to Seb on the other side of the alley. He leaned out and also looked for attackers.

Seb hadn't given them explicit instructions, but he saw the Shadow Order soldiers divide equally and spread out. Each team picked a warehouse to hide behind. The hammer of their feet, although muted with their caution, still called out to any listening ears.

A tight grip on his weapon, Seb looked in the opposite direction to Bruke at his other friends. They all seemed ready and in control. Before they'd landed, he couldn't have guessed how long they'd have before they were attacked. Now, as he heard the stampede heading their way, he suddenly realised he thought they'd have had longer.

CHAPTER 8

They might have had strong fences on either side of them, preventing an attack from their flanks, but the weak chain-link netting over the end of each alley didn't seem up to much. After hearing their approach, Seb saw the front-runners of the chaotic mob heading their way. Despite them doing what he'd hoped they would, dread sank through him to watch them close down on the weak fence. Too late to back out now.

A second later, the loud splash of it yielding rang out as the crazed stampede rushed through it without breaking stride. Similar splashes ran down the other two alleys, almost impossible to discern amongst the screaming insanity.

A wall of maybe fifty of them in his alley, Seb looked at their attackers. Mandulus, grints, snirks, the porcupine things they'd seen running the Countess' slavery business ... and a whole host more. *Remember,* Seb said to his friends, *as intimidating as they look, they're victims. They haven't chosen this fight.*

None of them replied.

Zero organisation in the attacking mob, they filled the

alley as they charged down it. The creatures were dressed poorly on account of being slaves. No doubt they'd been treated terribly, toughened up by sadistic masters; they had every right to be furious.

The collective screams and roars swelled in the tight space, amplified by the high walls.

Seb knew the others were watching him, waiting for him to make a move. A deep breath; they had to get this over with. He stepped from cover and opened fire, spraying rubber bullets up the alley.

The gun kicked more than a blaster would, the vibration of it rattling Seb's vision as he unloaded into the beasts. Many of the soldiers from the boats were still getting into position, so they couldn't provide backup yet.

The first assault slowed their attackers, the creatures flinching and covering their faces from the stinging onslaught. But they still came forward. Because he'd had a few seconds of exposure to them and the advantage of viewing it in slow motion, it allowed Seb to assess their enemy. Some of the beasts had weapons of their own. The ones without blasters carried clubs or swords.

"Take cover!" Seb yelled as a barrage of laser fire flooded forward. As he pulled back, he watched the green, red, blue, and yellow blasts shoot across the open space between them and the sea.

When Seb peered around the wall again, he saw the creatures continued to stream into the alley. What had been about fifty looked to have doubled already. Another line of blasts rushed at him, so he pulled back and watched the lasers fly towards the sea again.

More Shadow Order soldiers got into position. Seb looked to his right and saw a laser smash into the face of one of the rookies who'd exposed themselves too early. An explosion of red mist burst out of the back of its head, turning it instantly flaccid. One of the other Shadow Order creatures yelled, "We have to use lasers."

"No," Seb called, his order lost in the chaos of the battle. The Shadow Order soldiers returned fire with lasers rather than rubber bullets. *SA,* he said, *I need your help here. Can you put me through to everyone?*

Sure.

This is Seb, he said and watched the confusion on many faces. *Don't worry about how I'm in your head, just take cover and listen. These creatures are* victims. *It's Enigma who's made them this way. We need to keep using rubber bullets. We need to take them down and put them somewhere secure. I'm hoping we can find a way to help them.*

Although many of the creatures stared at Seb like he'd lost his mind, none of them argued. They'd all been briefed. They knew the drill.

A scream erupted just metres from Seb, dragging his focus back to the alley. He had just enough time to raise his weapon before the beast emerged. A foot taller and wider than him, it fixed him with its Cyclops eye. The thing looked like a corpse, its skin a wrinkly mummified mess, its blue eye sunken in its face, its mouth toothless. When it shrieked, its voice ran so shrill it sent searing needles through Seb's ears and unsettled his balance. It wielded a large scimitar, gripping the handle with both hands as it cut through the air as if to decapitate him.

Seb ducked at the last moment, his aggressor's weapon sailing over his head and smashing against the metal corner of the warehouse. A shower of sparks rained down on him. Although he watched the creature in slow motion, he saw no weak spot. Then he looked at its feet. Its vulnerability rested there.

While the creature wound back for another swing, slow because of its size, Seb drove his metal fist against the top of its left foot. His blow went straight through it, clearly turning every bone to dust. The beast shrieked again.

Seb punched the other foot. It dropped its weapon and fell to the ground, holding onto its feet while yelling with all it had.

A second later, a dart flew into the beast, turning it instantly limp. When Seb looked behind at SA, he nodded his thanks and returned his attention to the alley and the bulk of their attackers. What had seemed like an overwhelming number of creatures looked to have doubled again. More blaster fire rushed at them, more screams of aggression, more fury.

To look down the alley for too long would be to lose his head to a blast, so Seb pulled back, poked his gun around the corner, and sent another barrage of rubber bullets at the creatures. Unless he aimed at the sky, chances were he'd hit something.

Screams all around him, Seb heard some coming from the mouths of the Shadow Order soldiers. They were mostly rookies. If the rest were to survive, they needed more guidance than he'd given them so far.

Take cover, Seb said through SA. *We can take these down if we stay organised. Get your machine guns ready, and on my count, we'll lay down fire. Three ... two ... now.*

As Seb moved out into the alley with a group of soldiers around him, he sent another stream of rubber bullets into their aggressors. More fire came from those on Bruke's side. Enough of an onslaught, it knocked the front line of their attackers down and drove the entire pack back.

Now take cover, Seb yelled. A quick check along the line,

he looked at his friends: SA, Sparks, Bruke, and Owsk. They all nodded at him.

That's it, Seb said to everyone. *And again. Three ... two ... now.*

They did the same again. They drove their attackers back even farther this time.

Three ... two ... now.

Although the next attack worked as well as the other two, opening up a bit more space between them and the insanity rushing at them, Seb felt something shake through the ground, and he froze. When he peered down the alley at what could be coming their way, he couldn't see for the black smoke from the burning ships. Another thud. In stereo this time. He might not have known what species came towards them, but from the sounds, he knew there were more than one. He knew they were gargantuan.

What the hell is that noise? Sparks said.

Before Seb could reply, they burst through the smoke. The sight of them forced gasps and screams from his brothers and sisters around him. The creatures looked to be made from rock like Owsk, but they were four times the size of him, at least. Trolls like he'd never seen before. Thirty of them, if not more. They moved more slowly than their smaller attackers, but they looked no less insane and taken over with Enigma's fury. Rubber bullets wouldn't do anything against them.

Retreat, Seb said. *If we can avoid killing them, we should. They've done nothing wrong. We can always come back when we're better armed.*

"It's them or us," a rookie on Seb's right shouted at him as it drew its blaster.

"No!" Seb called, thrusting a halting hand in its direction. "Get back to the ships and out to sea. There has to be a way to take them down without killing them."

The rookie looked at him like it didn't trust what he'd said, but it had clearly been trained well enough to take an order. It and all of those around it retreated while Seb held his position, sending another barrage of rubber bullets down the alley without looking. He had to let the others get to safety before he went himself.

The emergence of the giant trolls had galvanised their aggressors, and they charged forwards again. Another wave of blaster fire came at the Shadow Order's retreat from the three alleys, bursting out into the open space beyond.

A glance to his left, Seb saw the white-skinned creature that had been on the boat with him. It hid behind the warehouse on its own. Bruke had already retreated. "What are you doing?" Seb called across at it.

"You can't fight them on your own," the creature shouted back.

"I'm not going to fight them. I just want to give the others a chance to escape."

"I'm staying with you."

Seb poked his head around the warehouse and looked down the alley at the advancing army. After pulling his head back again, he opened fire from behind the cover of the building.

As their attackers returned rubber with lasers, Seb saw most of his army had now retreated. He called at the white-skinned creature, "We're going now!"

The pallid beast stepped away from its warehouse too.

His back to the attacking army as he sprinted away from them, Seb watched some of the boats racing out to sea as he got closer to the water. His friends stood there without a ship. "What's happened?" he called at them.

Sparks threw her arms in the air. "They panicked and took all the boats." She spat on the ground. "Damn rookies."

Seb and the white-skinned creature caught up to them and stopped. The Shadow Order soldiers seemed oblivious to those they'd left behind as they retreated. A glance back at the warehouses showed the slaves rushing from the alleys, with blasters, swords, and bats in hands.

"We've got to use our blasters," Buster said.

Even with the insanity twisting the creatures' faces—masks of horror charging their way—Seb saw their innocence. They were like wild animals. They were panicking, nothing more. None of this was their fault. Hell, he'd nearly been one of them. "But it's such a waste."

"It's them or us," Buster said.

As more and more creatures appeared, pushing the seven of them back towards the sea, Seb still couldn't give the order. There had to be a better way.

CHAPTER 9

"Look out!" the white-skinned creature yelled as it ran at Seb. The brief moment Seb had spent not in slow motion passed, his gift kicking in to show him every gruesome detail as it unfolded.

The pallid rookie leaped towards him with its arms spread wide. Its red eyes fixed on him as it travelled through the air. A second later, it clattered into him, hitting him hard around his upper body, sending both of them to the ground.

The creature filled the space where Seb had been just seconds ago. It took the wave of blaster fire intended for him. Red, green, blue, and yellow lasers tore into the rookie's body, shaking it with the impact, its blood spraying away from it in a wash of green.

Seb took the weight of them both as a stinging blow to his right shoulder against the concrete ground. The pressure of the rookie's body drove the air from his lungs. Not quite dead, the rookie looked down through its small red eyes. Green blood leaked from the laser holes it had been filled with, a trickle of it running down his face.

An emerald teardrop formed on the end of the creature's

nose. Before it dripped, Seb rolled the body off him. The oily consistency of its spilled essence coated his fingers. He wiped its hair away from its forehead, leaving a wide swipe of green against its pale complexion.

Immediately after they'd been shot at, Sparks and SA stepped forward, opening up on their attackers with a spray of rubber bullets. Although it drove those in the front back by a few steps, Sparks said what Seb knew to be true. "We can't hold them back for much longer. We need a better plan than the one we're using."

Still on the ground, Seb looked back into the rookie's small red eyes. It gasped for breath as it clung onto life, its green blood pooling around it. "Next time—" it said and took a breath "—one of the rookies looks like they're going to drown ... leave them. You're too important."

Seb shook while holding onto the kid. Because he'd made a decision to save those attacking them by returning fire with rubber bullets, soldiers had died. Whatever choice he made, beings had to die, and he couldn't continue to sacrifice those fighting beside him. Those willing to die for him.

The boy then fell limp. After clearing the lump in his throat, Seb said to those around him, "We need to switch to blasters."

The instruction they'd been waiting for, Bruke, Owsk, and Buster all unslung their semi-automatic weapons. A glance out at those on the boats floating in the sea, the chance to speak to them through SA remained open. Seb said, *We're switching to live weapons now. Put the rubber bullets down and drive this lot back. We've given them every opportunity to save their lives. Now we need to save ours.*

A roar of engines from the boats in the sea, Seb watched them come back into land, blasters in hand rather than their machine guns. Those not driving the boats pointed their weapons towards the shore.

The kid's head still in his hands, Seb stared at it for a few seconds before he let it rest against the concrete. His five closest friends between him and the slaves, they laid down enough fire to keep their attackers momentarily at bay.

Seb got to his feet and dragged the rookie's dead body to the edge of the water, kissed him on the forehead, and slipped him in. He shouldn't have died. No other creature would fall because of his inaction.

After he'd watched the kid vanish from sight, Seb pulled his blaster free, raised it to his shoulder, and looked at the three alleys. The others had them covered, bodies piling up from where their attackers were dropped the second they showed their faces.

Seb joined the line of his friends and spoke to everyone in his army. *We need to drive these back and reclaim Aloo. Hopefully we can save some of them in the process, but we can't put ourselves in harm's way to do it.*

The pulse of the rifle ran through Seb's body, shaking his torso with its rapid fire. He helped drop the possessed slaves as quickly as they appeared. One or two got wildly inaccurate shots off in return, but many of them were taken down before they could even do that.

Hard to watch the creatures fall, but Seb continued to shoot them the second they appeared. He could have been one of them and understood what they'd been through better than most, but he had to protect his people, and they had to take Aloo back.

The crunch of the boats slid onto the concrete behind them for a second time. Seb and his closest friends all stepped forward to make room. The soldiers from the water widened their line of attack as they joined the fight on either side. The slaves didn't stand a chance.

But they continued to fight, more and more of them bursting from the alleys. Their screams exploded from the tight walkways with them. Many of them were silenced before they had fully let loose their battle cries. It didn't stop them. Their fear and paranoia were bigger motivators than self-preservation.

Although many of the Shadow Order's blasts landed and slowed down the slaves' advances, many missed. Sparks kicked off the metal corners that sleeved the warehouse's walls. Chips of brick exploded away from the blasts that crashed into the masonry.

Had their aggressors had any thoughts in their heads other than to attack, they might have used their advantage better. They'd driven the Shadow Order out into the open, and they had cover to shoot from. But they continued to rush out of the alleys with just one thing on their mind: the destruction of those they perceived to be a threat.

Then they stopped. The chaos in the alleys quieted. They were still there, but they weren't coming forward anymore. Maybe they could save some of them. Maybe Enigma's programming could be tamed. "They've realised they can't win," Seb said to his friends in a whisper. With a relieved sigh, he smiled for those they'd save. "At last!"

In the heat of the battle, Seb had forgotten about them. When he felt the ground shake with their slow and steady approach, he looked down the line at his friends. They all looked back at him. It took for Sparks to say it. "Or maybe they're just standing aside for those giant trolls."

CHAPTER 10

Not only had his five closest friends noticed the vibrations running through the ground, but when Seb looked at the Shadow Order army on either side of him, he saw they'd all stopped shooting too. Some were even stepping back towards the boats they'd just come in on. *Hold your positions,* he said to them. *We have live ammo now; that has to count for something.*

The looks that came back at Seb showed him many of them didn't share his confidence, including Sparks, who said, "We need something better than lasers if we're going to take *them* down. You saw them, right?"

The sound of the giant trolls barrelled through the alleys, their heavy slathering breaths a rumble in the tight spaces. They were unrelenting in their forward momentum, the vibrations through the ground getting so heavy it felt like the concrete would crack.

Although Seb wrapped a tight grip around his gun, he had no idea what he'd do with it. Despite what he'd said to the others, Sparks was right: their blasts would bounce off the trolls as if they were rubber bullets. They needed something nuclear to take the oafs down.

The rumble of the trolls' breaths and the earthquake running through their feet melded into one. They were going to roll right over Seb and his army if he didn't do something.

Despite not looking back at the Shadow Order soldiers, it didn't mean Seb didn't have an awareness of all the beings' attention on him. They needed guidance. But with no military training, how did they expect him to come up with a strategy?

The rumble grew louder still.

Because he had no other choice, Seb stepped towards the alleys. He could be a leader. At least he had that in him.

A whine in his voice showed Bruke's anxiety when he said, "What are you doing?"

"Someone needs to meet them head-on. Maybe when I get closer, I can work out a way to take them down."

Although Bruke whined again, he offered nothing more by way of response. Seb took off and ran to the closest warehouse.

When he got to the nearest building—tens of dead slaves at his feet—Seb pressed his back against the wall and felt the earthquake shake of the approaching trolls.

Having only seen them from a distance, Seb drew a deep breath before he peered down the alley closest to him. He froze when he saw the first troll. So wide, it took up the entire walkway and had at least three more behind it. Grey-skinned like Owsk, it looked to be made from rock like him too. A slow-motion view of the creature, if it had a weak spot, he couldn't see it and probably didn't have the strength to exploit it either. He'd need a jackhammer to even make a dent in the thing.

Although small compared to them, Seb didn't go unnoticed. The thing stared down at him through large black eyes.

Cold and detached, when it opened its mouth, it revealed a cave of red capable of swallowing him whole. As it drew a breath, it pulled Seb from his hiding place. When it roared, the expulsion of air threw him back like a leaf in a hurricane.

Robbed of his cover, Seb rolled over several times before he came to a halt in the middle of the expanse of concrete between the warehouses and the sea. It afforded him a view down all three alleys at once. A troll led the line in each of them, splashes of blood bursting from beneath their feet as they crushed the dead bodies in their path. All three of them had others behind them, each line a death train travelling with the force of a natural disaster.

Nothing for it, Seb spoke to the army while remaining seated. *We can't do anything against them*—but before he could finish, he heard them.

Seb turned around to watch a line of chrome mechs land behind him. The slam of their touching down halted even the trolls. Eight in total, each of them stood larger than even the tallest of the rocky giants in the alleys.

As Seb scrambled to his feet, he watched the mechs form a protective line between the rest of the Shadow Order army and their attackers.

The trolls yelled, their roars shaking off the warehouses' walls on either side of them. The whir of the mechs arming themselves met their cries. Guns burst from shiny chrome arms and turned fists into Gatling guns.

What are you doing? SA said to Seb.

Despite the trolls being distracted, Seb hadn't moved. Before he could set off, he heard a *thwoom* and then a hiss of chains. The rush of air knocked him to the ground again as a projectile flew over his head. From where he sat, he watched the large metal cargo net catch the troll and send it stumbling back into the alley with the others behind it. Not only that, but the net clung to the walls on either side, pinning them in like a spider's web.

Two other mechs loosed their nets, sealing each alley with the trolls still inside them.

As one, the mechs leapt into the air and flew over the top of the warehouses. While getting to his feet for a second time, Seb listened to them land on the other side and loose another series of nets.

The sound of several more projectiles rang out. A different noise than the chains, more a pop than a whoosh. A few seconds later, yellow gas rose from the ground and started to fill the alleys.

One of the mechs came back over and landed in front of Seb. It hit the ground so hard, it flipped him like a pea on a drum.

With a *whoosh* of hydraulics, the front of the large vessel opened to reveal Reyes. She smiled, her happiness quickly fading when she looked down at the dead bodies on the ground. Some were Shadow Order soldiers, although they were mostly slaves. "Sorry we didn't get to you sooner. We had to wait for the lasers to stop firing in the sky. We wouldn't have made it in against those anti-air cannons."

Before Seb could reply, Reyes looked out at the rest of the Shadow Order army, winking when she made eye contact with Sparks. When she spoke, her suit amplified her voice so the army could hear her. "We have this under control now. They can't get out of the alleys, and the gas will knock them out cold for hours. You should all get back to the base before the gas hits you."

But none of them moved. It took a few seconds for Seb to see they were all staring at him. *Well done,* he said to them, still talking through SA. *We fought a hard and well-won battle. There were more casualties than there should have been on both sides, but I think we have most of the chaos contained now. The mechs will do a sweep of the port. It shouldn't be too much more work to reclaim Aloo. Now we need to get on the boats and head back to the Shadow Order's base. There are many more places that need our help.*

As the army pulled back, Reyes nodded at Seb. "You did us proud."

"We wouldn't have finished it without you. And next time I could do with you beside me; I know nothing about the tactics of war."

Shrugging, Reyes said, "I think you did okay." She saluted him. "Well done, sir."

Although he saw the sincerity in her gesture, it meant nothing to him. Too many had died. Still, he nodded and said, "Thank you." And with that, he headed back to one of the boats with the others. They might have Aloo back under control, but they had a hell of a lot more work ahead of them.

CHAPTER 11

Where the conference room in the Shadow Order's base had been laid out so Moses could stand at the front and deliver his knowledge, he'd since rearranged it, clearing many of the chairs to one side and leaving the few remaining laid out in a circle. It gave Seb a view of all the beings around him. Maybe Moses saw them all as equals now. Even if he didn't, it looked like he wanted to give that impression.

Seb shivered again. No matter how many times he'd asked him, Moses never lifted the temperature of the room. Although, none of the others complained about it, so maybe Moses never had cause to. Why should their environment be set to meet the needs of just one individual? Seb could always put a coat on. A look at the others, they all stared back at him as he went around the circle. Owsk, Buster, SA, Sparks, Reyes, Bruke, Moses, and Mr. H.

Moses finally broke the silence. "Well done, all of you. You took Aloo back."

"Yeah, but what now?" Owsk said, many of the others nodding at his question, including Seb.

When Moses returned silence, it showed he didn't have a plan either. He looked around the room as if hoping for one of them to deliver some insight.

After another few seconds of silence, Sparks broke it by pulling out her computer and projecting footage on the wall at the front. Screams, cries, gunfire, and even a distant explosion or two, she showed them the reality of the chaos. "What we have to face hasn't changed. There's anarchy everywhere else; so while getting Aloo back might be a small achievement, it's no more than that."

Moses shrugged. "But it's important. At least we have our base secured. It's something. It gives us a location to regroup in so we can execute our next plan."

"Which is?" Sparks said. All the while she kept her attention on her minicomputer, cycling through the footage every few seconds. The scenery changed with her swipes. Open agricultural land, built-up cities, run-down shanty towns— very different settings, exactly the same chaos.

Hard to take his eyes from the footage, Seb winced as he watched a being forced to its knees before several creatures dressed in the rags of slaves hacked its head off with a sword. Unlike the glorified beheadings he'd seen in movies, it took more than one swing to decapitate the poor thing.

When Seb looked back, he saw the others had watched it too. A shuttle crash they couldn't look away from, they all wore their own masks of horror. "Any ideas on how we can get closer to Enigma?" he said.

An already all too familiar silence settled on the room. Sparks then said, "The longer it takes us to find out where they are, the more beings will die. It seems to me that the only plan we have is to take back one planet at a time. But we don't have the might for that."

"And the chaos will spread quicker than we can quell it," Reyes added.

While nodding her agreement with the marine, Sparks turned back to the others. "We have to come up with something else."

Because he had nothing to offer, Seb continued to watch Sparks' projected footage. "Another thing bothering me," he said, "is how they got so organised on Aloo."

Sparks looked between Seb and the footage several times. "Huh?"

"The slaves. When I look at them on other planets, they seem to be operating without purpose. They're attacking anything close by. But when we turned up in Aloo, they all came at us."

"Like they were working together," Buster said.

"Exactly."

Sparks shook her head. "They weren't working together. Aloo looked just like all of these other places until we turned up. When we did, we became the greatest threat to their safety, which is why they came at us in that way. I would argue that although the slaves were all drawn to Moses' warehouses as a group, they were acting as single entities. Just look at the way they came out to be slaughtered ... there was no co-ordination there."

It made sense, so Seb nodded. "Fair point." Not that it got them any closer to a plan. "So what do we do, then?"

Where's the hostage?

Seb noticed Owsk and Buster flinch at SA's voice coming through to them. They still hadn't gotten used to it. "She has a point," he said. "We should be pressing him for answers. Especially as we have nothing else at the moment."

Buster leaned forward and spoke in a low growl. "I'll be more than happy to torture it."

Seb shuddered at his tone. The rest of the room fell silent.

"What?" A shrug of his shoulders, Buster looked at the others. "I just thought I'd offer my services."

Silence again, which Seb broke a second later. "Although the creature can't tell us anything, it won't deny it if we guess correctly. It might be a long process, but it has to be the best option we have. Is he nearby, Moses?"

The large shark nodded. "I'll take you to him."

~

Moses led the way down one of the Shadow Order base's many identical gunmetal grey corridors. Seb fell into line with the others, the only sound coming from the contact their feet made against the steel floor.

When they arrived at one of what appeared to be hundreds of identical doorways, Moses paused and looked back at them. "I've kept it too bright and too cold for the creature to sleep in. Hopefully the little shit is so exhausted, he'd sell his own mother up the river just to get some rest."

Before anyone could comment, Moses pressed his face to the retina scanner by the door. Seb watched the light turn from red to green. A second later, the door lock clicked before the entire thing opened with a whirring sound.

The bright glare flooding out forced Seb back a couple of steps, and he raised his forearm to cover his eyes. It took a few seconds for his vision to adjust. When it did, he said, "Oh no."

The porcupine sat at the other end of the room. About three metres separated him and Seb. His voice ran shrill, a wobble to it as if forming the words took all of his resolve. "Stay where you are," he said.

Although the others crowded around behind him, Seb

remained still and raised his hands as if urging the small beast to calm down. "I'm not moving." He stared into the creature's wild eyes. It looked sleep deprived, sure, but something else drove him. Maybe the threat of a punishment more severe than anything the Shadow Order would even dream of doing to him.

The small creature kneeled as if praying. It had pulled two thick spines from itself and had one up each nostril. It shook its head as it rested its palms on the floor and shouted, "Don't come any closer." Spittle sprayed from its violent outburst.

"Now calm down," Seb said, the others letting him take the lead. "Just don't do anything rash, okay?"

Another shake of its head swung the spines from side to side as an elongated extension of the creature's actions. "I'm not giving you anything more about Enigma."

Before Seb could say anything else, the creature shouted, its voice echoing in the empty room, "You're all going to hell! Long live Enigma." It yelled out as it drove a head butt at the ground. The sharp spikes vanished inside its skull with a deep crunch. The creature fell instantly limp, the weight of its body shoving its face along the floor towards them. Within a few seconds, blood leaked from its nose and pooled around it.

"Damn!" Sparks said as she elbowed her way to the front. She ran a hand over the top of her head, pulling her black bob from her face and holding it there while she exhaled hard. "There goes our hostage."

CHAPTER 12

They were all back in the conference room and had returned to their seats. In the same seats as before, they wore the same blank expressions. None of them had spoken on the walk back.

Buster finally broke the silence, leaning forward and eyeballing Seb. "*You're* supposed to be the chosen one."

"What do you mean by that?"

"Surely you know something?"

"I didn't choose this damn prophecy."

Silence again.

Sparks brought up more footage of the chaos incited by Enigma. It looked like she did it through boredom rather than any particular reason. "This is Zackint," she said. "The closest planet to us."

While watching it, Seb shrugged. "It could be anywhere in the galaxy right now." The same scenes they'd seen everywhere. Uncoordinated, wild, and destructive creatures fell while buildings and ships burned.

Suddenly, an image flashed into Seb's mind. Although he flinched, he kept his response muted. He saw a tower of some sort. A monument. A tall milky-green obelisk. After a shake of his head, he looked across at SA, who stared straight at him. Had she just put the thought in his head? Blood then ran from her nose like it had before, and her skin turned paler than usual. This time, he lurched forward to catch her from her seat as she fell.

CHAPTER 13

The others gathered around Seb, who held SA in his arms and looked down at her. Moses had given him some tissues to wipe her blood away with. Only a nosebleed, but it spoke of something much more. While lowering her gently to the ground so she could stretch out, he stared into her blue eyes. A slight glaze to her bioluminescence, the clarity soon returned as she focused on him. Something in her stare suggested she knew he'd seen it too. Had they seen exactly the same thing? He checked his own nose by pushing the back of his hand against it. No blood.

It took until that moment for Seb to truly feel the press of his friends around them. Their collective forms blocked out a lot of the room's light. He looked up at them, trying to keep his impatience from his tone. "Can you please give her some space? She needs room to breathe."

The others backed away. It took for that moment to see Sparks hadn't been there in the first place. As always, she stared down at her device, and maybe with just cause. "Look," she said as she sent yet another projection onto the wall.

The footage showed the same chaos they'd seen all over the galaxy already. Had she just done it to take the attention away from SA?

Before Seb could ask her, she said, "See how they're behaving. It's different than before."

Like the others in the room, Seb watched the chaos while holding SA's hand. "It doesn't look any different. The same killing, the same insanity."

"Look harder."

Torn between Sparks' riddles and the woozy SA, Seb threw an impatient shrug through his shoulders. "Why don't you just tell me?"

Sparks pointed at the projected footage again. "Look at how they're running around. Before, they were acting on their own, attacking on their own. There was no organisation to the madness, even when they attacked us on Aloo. But look at them now."

The current destination on the screen was a shanty town of tin roofs, poorly built buildings, and tents. It looked much like the slums of Solsans. It showed the slaves grouping together in packs. Bruke spoke this time. "Maybe something's attracted their attention like we did on Aloo."

Shaking her head, Sparks cycled through zoomed-in shots of the creatures in the slum. "But they're not going anywhere in particular. They're grouping into larger packs and killing those who aren't like them. Look." She showed more footage of seven or eight slaves as they closed down on a large creature and threw it to the ground. Dressed better than they were, it clearly came from wealth.

As they closed in around their victim, Seb winced. He squirmed where he sat, and just before he could say something, Owsk beat him to it. "Do we have to watch this?"

But Sparks didn't reply, and no one turned away. It

twisted Seb's insides to watch the group quickly beat the creature to death. As much as he didn't want to witness it, the small Thrystian had made the correct call: they needed to understand the phenomena.

The violent gang left the corpse on the ground and ran over to a group of a similar size to their own. Not even acknowledging one another, they instantly doubled in size as a unit and moved on, searching for their next target.

Seb noticed Sparks looking around the room before she said, "I take your silence to mean you can see my point?"

More silence. It felt as if the footage had dragged the air from the room and the breath from their lungs.

"Maybe I'm stating the obvious here," Sparks said, "but with the change that's just occurred, I think we've got even less time before every planet's overrun." She cycled through more footage. The same thing. Organised chaos. "The last time SA collapsed—"

"Was shortly after Enigma triggered the attack," Seb said. He felt SA look at him. Did she want a confirmation that he'd seen it too? He ignored her. If she had projected it into his mind, she didn't need the stress of worrying about it happening again. If she hadn't, he didn't want to discuss it until he understood it more.

Even Bruke picked up on what they were saying. "So you think Enigma have triggered a change in the slaves' behaviour and SA picked up on the psychic broadcast?"

"Exactly," Sparks said. "It must have been some kind of psychic output that created this, much like the thing that triggered the chaos in the first place."

Because Seb had his attention on the others, he jumped when SA sat up and held her head. She winced as if she had a headache. *I saw something. A place. A monument.*

It had to be what Seb had seen. He let her speak.

A large obelisk. It was milky green as if made from jade. It had carvings on it, but I can't remember what they were. They looked like religious symbols of some sort.

Exactly the same thing he'd seen.

Sparks flicked through a couple of cities' monuments as if searching for what she'd just described.

SA pointed at the screen when it flashed up. *That's it.*

A large green obelisk, it stood at least three metres tall. The city surrounding it had lights everywhere. It looked to be night-time because the sky was dark while the ground was lit up like the sun from the artificial illumination.

"Kajan," Sparks said.

Bruke leaned towards her. "Huh?"

"SA saw the Pillar of Peace in the centre of Kajan's main square. It's a secular society. They celebrate the fact with an obelisk carved from jade. Those symbols on it are the main religious symbols when it was made. They wanted to welcome every faith. Of course, thousands of religions have been birthed and died since it was made, but its message remains: all faiths are welcome. None rule."

A slight dryness crept through Seb's mouth, and his heart pounded to watch the insanity in the city. What had been disorganised chaos had seemed like his worst nightmare before this. Now they'd be facing a hive mind moving through the place like a plague of locusts. Systematic in their destruction, they left fire and devastation in their wake.

"It looks worse than any other place we've seen," Bruke said.

"It's a busy city," Sparks said. "A population of about fifty thousand beings, the place is built on gambling and prostitution. It isn't pretty down there at the best of times."

"Forget it." Buster stood up, his tail flicking in an aggressive display of his fear. "I ain't going."

Seb cut in this time. "We can't force you to do anything you don't want to, Buster. I need to go there, so maybe we should focus on who's coming with me."

Although she'd sat up, SA still leaned on Seb for support. She raised her hand. Reyes, Bruke, and Sparks followed suit. When they all looked at Owsk, the rock troll shrugged. "I'm guessing Buster's going to need some help looking after the slaves on Aloo. Maybe we can put out a broadcast to send them here if any beings have any they need to offload. Being surrounded by the sea makes it the perfect place to contain them until we can find something that'll help."

It might have been a coward's answer, but it made sense. Besides, Seb only wanted beings who'd chosen to be there next to him. The city they were about to go to had already fallen. The last thing he needed was resistance from his team on top of everything else. As he watched the footage of Kajan, he felt more aware of his fatigue than ever. His blood ran like tar through his veins while a low-level pain buzzed in his muscles. Although he knew it for himself, he said to SA, "Are you sure that's the monument you saw?"

As much as she looked like she wanted to say no, she nodded. *Certain.*

"Well, at least that's something," Seb said, doing his best to hide his disappointment. "At least we know where we need to go. Buster, Owsk, we'll put out a call in case any ships have slaves they need to drop off here. Good luck. The rest of you, I suppose there's no time like the present." When he stood up, he offered SA his hand to help her stand too. A look at the rest of the team and they all returned his stare with stoic determination. About to ask them if they were ready, he saw he didn't need to. Instead, he pulled in a deep breath and said, "Let's do this."

CHAPTER 14

Their ship shook and hummed as they entered Kajan's atmosphere. Seb lost his breath to see the vast sprawling city in the middle of the dark desert. The night gave them no choice but to focus on the neon metropolis. Tower block after tower block, the city had been arranged in grids. Many of the skyscrapers burned. Turned into chimneys, they kicked up thick smoke into the dark sky.

Suddenly Reyes turned the ship's lights off.

"What are you doing?" Seb said. He stood behind her in the cockpit, holding onto her seat. An ache ran through his knuckles from how tightly he gripped it.

Although Reyes kept her attention in front, she leaned back and spoke to him over her shoulder. "You want us to announce our arrival? If we go in lit up, they'll spot us before we land."

"Why does it matter?" Bruke said. "We'll be visible on radar anyway."

Her focus still ahead, and not aggressive in any way, Reyes shut him down nonetheless. "Any being that can use radar down there won't give a damn about us turning up. They'll be too busy trying to hide."

As usual, Sparks had her attention on her computer. "I bet there aren't any beings left who can use radar anyway. The ones who might be capable look like they're making their way out into the desert." She pointed at a map on her screen. It showed a large cluster of dots in the city and then a scattering of activity far out in the desert in every direction. The lucky ones had managed to flee before it was too late.

A moment's silence as they all watched what they were heading into, Reyes then broke it. "The point is, we want to land without anything seeing or hearing us." She then reached forward and flicked a switch on the dashboard. The vibration of the ship's engines suddenly stopped.

Seb looked at the others before addressing Reyes. "What the hell?"

In the co-pilot seat, still locked on her computer, Sparks looked out of the window in front of them for a second before returning to her screen. "They might hear us. We can glide in from here."

Despite Seb's inclination to argue with them, they both knew more about flying than he did. Besides, if he kicked off now, it would just make a tricky landing much trickier.

In the absence of the humming engines, Seb heard the wind resistance around the ship. It served as a reminder of just how fast they were hurtling towards the ground. For a moment, he closed his eyes and inhaled deeply. It took for SA to reach over and squeeze his right hand before he opened them again. She offered him a tight-lipped smile, which he returned.

Sparks then projected an image on the windscreen much like the one she'd brought up when they'd rescued their friends from the snowy mountain. Like before, it showed a red-lined schematic of the obstacles in their path.

Still no replacement for actually being able to see, Seb looked out at the city again. Now they were closer, he saw the flames around the bottoms of many buildings. One or two of the towers had already fallen, a large pile of rubble where they'd clearly been, their skeletal remains still smoking. The lights and flames glowed so brightly, he had to rub his eyes to help combat the glare. "So, what?" he said. "We land at night, find somewhere to hide, and then go into the city when we have some daylight?"

"There is no daylight," Sparks said without looking back at him.

"Say what?"

While still facing forward, Sparks said, "There. Is. No. Daylight."

"It's always dark?"

"Not exactly dark though, is it?"

"All right, smart arse. So it's always retina-burning bright? As long as you're in the artificially lit city?"

"Yep."

The words of his mother came to Seb at that moment, reminding him he had nothing nice to say. He pulled in another deep breath and slowly let it go. What else could he do?

The numbers on the screen in front of them meant nothing to Seb, but they must have told Reyes something. After frowning at them, she said, "We're going to be landing soon."

Tight-lipped, Seb listened to Bruke whine next to him and continued to hold SA's hand as they descended towards Kajan's barren desert. He looked at his love to see the colour had returned to her face. She appeared to be strong again and as ready as any of them.

Suddenly, the ship jolted with a loud *bang!*

Instantly in slow motion, Seb let go of SA's hand and held the back of Reyes' seat again. "What the hell was that?"

Bang! They hit something else, the ship jumping higher like a skipped stone.

The dashboard of the ship lit up like the city in front of them. The pulse and bleep of several warning signals went off. No one replied to Seb, Reyes holding onto the flight stick with both hands as their ship snaked from side to side.

Bang! Another bone-shuddering vibration and Seb nearly lost his feet as they swung into a death spin.

"What's going on, Sparks?" Reyes yelled, her teeth bared. She tugged so hard on the flight stick, she looked like she might rip it clean off.

Seb continued to grip the back of Reyes' seat, losing his balance as the bright city's lights repeatedly came into view and then disappeared again with their spin. He watched Sparks on her computer.

Bang! They hit something again. It caught their left wing, abruptly halting their spiral. It did nothing to slow them down.

Still gripping the flight stick, Reyes yelled, "Hold on!"

Seb's slow motion gave him the chance to look to his left at Bruke. He clung to Sparks' seat like he wanted to rip it free from its bolts. Then to his right at SA. She looked as calm as ever. Before he could speak again, the screech of metal ripped through the bottom of their ship. It sounded like they were scraping against rock. It sounded like the ground was chewing through their hull. A fireworks display of sparks kicked up from the bottom of their vessel.

They lifted for a second before crashing down again. The screeching through the bottom of the ship brought a heavy shudder with it. It turned Seb's view of the city into a wash of blurred lights.

After maybe a hundred metres of grinding against the ground, they finally came to a stop.

Not quite silence, but none of them spoke. Seb looked at the others. Wide-eyed, they all panted—all except SA. She stared calm bioluminescence at him as if she knew they'd be safe all along.

"Sorry," Sparks finally said, her voice small. "I forgot to set my scanner to detect rocks."

A balled fist, Seb looked at the back of her head. Not that he'd hit her, but he damn well felt like it. He bit back his scream. He had to let it go. Even a being as calculating as her made mistakes. He then said, "We need to get out of here sharpish. I'm guessing that landing just told the locals we're coming."

While holding her tablet in his direction, a splay of thousands of red dots in front of them, Sparks said, "It looks like they didn't notice. None of them are coming this way."

"Are you sure you're scanning for beings?"

A facetious smile, Sparks then looked at the others. "I think we just got away with it."

If Seb thought he'd felt angry with Sparks, when he looked at Reyes, he saw her staring daggers at her small co-pilot. She worked her jaw as she ground her teeth. Her face moved several times as if she struggled with getting her words out. She finally managed it. "Except—" she took a breath "—we no longer have a ship to fly out of here in."

"Let's look on the bright side," Sparks said. "We've landed, we're alive, and the creatures in Kajan don't know we're here. We can find a ship when we need to get out of the city."

CHAPTER 15

In the silence that followed Sparks' comment, Seb cautiously stood up and stretched. No pain in his body yet, but it would come. A crash-landing like the one they'd just been through always took its pound of flesh. The impact of the landing on top of the past few weeks he'd had would no doubt take even more than that.

Before anyone spoke, Seb heard Bruke sniffing, inquisitive in its nature. Seb watched his friend looking around the inside of their crashed ship.

When Seb smelled it too, dread crawled up through him as a strong and writhing twist. His heart quickened, and any breath he'd recovered from the crash ran away from him as he said, "I'm not imagining that smell, am I?"

Before Bruke could answer, Reyes jumped to her feet and yelled, "Get out!" She shooed Seb and Bruke out of the cockpit towards the back door and followed on their heels with Sparks.

No aches, but still reeling from the crash, the second Seb tried to run, he lost his balance, stumbled, and tripped, slamming down hard against the ship's metal floor. The team backing up behind him, he felt a shove from Bruke as he stood up for a second time before continuing towards the exit.

The power out and the ship twisted from the crash, Seb knew what would happen when he tried to open the door. But what other choice did he have? When he shoved it, it remained shut. The heady smell of fuel made him dizzy. One spark and they were done. He gritted his teeth and shoved it again. Still nothing.

No time for words, Bruke shoved Seb aside and shoulder barged the door. The metal panel flew away from the ship with the popping noise of a large cork, and the thickset lizard rode it out into the desert beyond, crashing down against the dusty ground.

They all ran out after him into the dark and cold.

The terrain uneven underfoot and no daylight to show them the way, Sparks took the lead, her computer in front of her as she used its torch to find a safe route. Hopefully, she'd checked for rocks this time.

As they ran, the ship behind them and the city in front, Seb looked at the illuminated metropolis, his breaths visible as condensation. He'd always associated deserts with heat, but why should this planet be warm? He should have worked it out. In a place where it was always night, how could it possibly be?

Not far behind Sparks, Seb watched her dart to the right. It took another moment before he saw the large rock she'd avoided. They all followed her, another rock in their way a second later. Were it not for the scattering of large boulders and stones, he would have had a much clearer view of the city beyond. But maybe he didn't need to get an idea of the full extent of what they were heading into. He didn't need anything challenging his desire to run as he fled a ship about to explode.

Despite what the rocks did to their line of sight, they did nothing to mute the sounds from the densely populated area ahead. Screams, cries, roars—the same insanity Seb had heard on Aloo. Torment, fury, chaos—what were they about to go into? Although, what part of the galaxy didn't have the same level of bedlam running through it? Wherever they went, they'd have to deal with it. Regardless of what went on, they had a plan to follow. Get to the pillar, find out what it could teach them, and then get the hell out of there.

After she'd rounded several more rocks, the others following her as they got away from their volatile ship, Sparks stopped and pulled out her computer. SA reached her first, then Seb, Reyes, and finally Bruke. The thickset creature might have been the first one out of the ship, but he didn't have a frame built for speed. Had they not stopped, he would have been left far behind.

While panting, Seb leaned in towards the others. They all sounded to be struggling like him. It had been non-stop for what felt like days now. When would it end? For a moment, no one spoke, the suffering in the city beyond filling the void. Now they were closer, he heard something else amongst the cries and shrieks. He heard sobbing. Broken and primal, whatever creatures made those noises, they sounded like they'd been to the end of what they could bear.

"This is where we need to go," Sparks said, pointing at the map on her screen with one long finger.

"Of course," Seb said, staring at the thick cluster of red dots beneath Sparks' fingertip. So many of them so close together, they looked like crimson frogspawn. "Why wouldn't we have to go where it's the busiest?"

"What did you expect? It's a monument that represents everything this place stands for. It's in the middle of the city's central plaza. They might not be thinking that clearly, but it makes sense that they'd return to their old ways, and if they're in some kind of second phase with a need to congregate, where else would they go?"

While Sparks talked, Seb watched her screen to see many more red dots far out of the city. He pointed at them. "Do you think they're survivors?"

A moment's pause, Sparks nodded. "Yeah."

"And you said the population on Kajan's about—"

"Fifty thousand," Sparks said.

"But there can't be any more than five thousand dots on your screen. At the most."

"My scanner doesn't pick up dead bodies."

In the following pause, more screams filled the night.

After she'd peered around the rock they crouched behind, then back in the direction they came from, Sparks said, "Well, at least the ship's—"

Before she could finish, a loud *thwoom* shook the ground as the ship ignited. The heat blast from the explosion rushed at them, tousling Seb's hair and instantly lifting sweat on his body. He looked into the sky at what had been the vessel they flew in on. Currently on fire, it had leapt about twenty metres, seemed to hover for a second, and then hurtled back down to earth, connecting with the ground with an almighty *clang!*

The explosion made Seb's ears ring. Had they been much closer to it, it would have deafened him. Although losing his hearing might have been for the better; that way, he wouldn't have to acknowledge the very real silence where there had been a cacophony of insanity only seconds before.

For the brief moment it lasted, Seb held his breath and looked at the others. All of them wore the same slack expression as if waiting for something else to happen. Before any of them spoke, the dark planet lit up with cries of chaos. This time it sounded like a shared chaos. An orchestrated chaos. Insanity with a purpose. And worst of all ... it headed straight for them.

CHAPTER 16

"We can make it if we go now," Sparks said, her intense stare flitting between her screen and Seb. "But we have to go *now*." When she tilted her computer to show him, he looked at the frogspawn of red dots headed their way. They were close, but not too close. Yet.

His world in slow motion, Seb had a moment or two longer than the others to think about it. It gave him the time to look at his friends. They all stared at him. In a moment of crisis, democracy went out of the window. He needed to make a decision. He nodded at Sparks. "Lead the way." Another glance at Bruke, who looked exhausted from what little running they'd already done, he added, "And we move at Bruke's pace. We either succeed or fail as a unit."

At that comment, the others drew their blasters as if readying for battle. Bruke whined, "You should go without me. I'll hide out here somewhere. Then there'll be no need to fight. You can get into the city and find somewhere safe. I can make my own way when the chaos clears. We don't all need to die because I'm slow."

Shaking his head, Seb pointed a stern finger at Bruke. "Shut up and get moving. We don't need to die because you're wasting our time moaning." A bit harsh, but it needed to be said.

The group set off, all of them running at a jog save for the huffing and puffing Bruke. The others looked over Sparks' shoulder, watching the dots get closer on her screen. The cries from inside the city gave them an audible marker to go with the visual in front of them.

When Seb saw SA had what looked to be a large grenade in her hand, he said, "What's that?"

Before SA could answer, Sparks looked down at it and gasped. "A leveller? Where did you get that from?"

I took it from Moses' armoury.

Reyes' eyes widened when she looked at it.

"Am I missing something?" Seb said.

Reyes continued to focus on the weapon. "A leveller does what it says on the tin. When it goes off, it reduces entire blocks to rubble."

Seb gulped. "Let's hope we don't need it."

Once they'd weaved through several more large rocks, Seb got his first clear sight of the city since he'd stepped out into the desert. Although he knew it to be bright when they approached from the sky, at ground level the brilliant neon glare exploded from the darkness like a supernova.

"Just go ahead without me," Bruke said between gasps. He already lagged behind them.

Seb ignored his stocky friend and looked down at Sparks' screen again, blinking several times before his eyes adjusted from the blinding the city had given him. So many red dots, he saw they bottlenecked and split, taking different paths from where the streets got too thin to accommodate them all.

Another round of screams, louder than before, he looked back at the garish sprawl of the city ahead. For the first time, he heard the thunderous swell of footsteps closing down on them.

Sparks' computer might have shown Seb that even the closest of the red dots still had a little way to go, but he found it hard to trust. Instead, he squinted as he scanned the line where the city met the desert for signs of emerging slaves. If Sparks had already failed to scan for rocks, who knew what else she might miss. Even a lone runner would blow their cover.

Despite him being a few steps behind, they still moved at Bruke's pace, their boots hitting the dusty ground. It gave Seb the chance to take in more of the city. It looked to be a work in progress. The grid layout had been clear from the sky, and as they drew closer, he saw where new grids had been started. If it survived this, it looked like Kajan would eventually grow in every direction to the horizon. Prostitutes and gambling must have been lucrative endeavours.

"I reckon we have about fifteen seconds," Sparks said, her small face flitting between her screen, the city, and the leveller in SA's hand.

When Seb looked back at Bruke, who'd lagged behind even farther, he saw the others do the same. Probably not helpful to the poor creature, he watched him wince an apology at them, but fortunately he didn't try to speak. It would be wasted energy. They wouldn't leave him, no matter how much he wanted them to.

A hotel stood as the closest building to them. At least fifteen stories high, every floor glowed from the bright electric lights inside it. A fire also burned within the tower. It looked like it had started on the second floor. Another glance up the tall building suggested the rooms above were empty.

Hopefully it had been evacuated in time. The chaos would have driven the guests out before the fires did.

The hotel stood as the first building in a new grid. It stood on its own; the next building was at least twenty metres farther away on the corner of a complete block.

The red frogspawn on Sparks' screen had split several more times. Clusters of creatures ran down the streets as a crimson flood. They moved towards the edge of the desert, divided by the architecture, but united in their hunt.

The thunder of footsteps had grown louder. The vibration of their stampede hammered through the streets and shook off the walls. Screams, shrieks, and cackles. Furious insanity. A lust for wanton destruction. It sounded like hell had broken open and the denizens contained within had burst free.

"We have to make a choice," Sparks said, her eyes fixed on the burning building. "I say we take our chances and go straight past that hotel."

When Seb looked at her screen, he saw they wouldn't make it to the next block. "I'll protect you from the fire," he said.

A slight stoop in her frame, Sparks clearly accepted what she'd said as wishful thinking. Were the hotel not on fire, she would have guided them straight to it. Hell, when he looked at her screen, Seb didn't know if they'd even make it to the burning structure.

The thud of their steps as they moved towards the blazing building, Seb continued to look between Sparks' computer and the illuminated city in front of them. The sounds drew closer, but still no sight of the insanity that created it.

A few metres between them and the hotel. The screams louder, the vibration of their footsteps harder. The hotel or bust. They had no choice.

Just before Seb ran through the smashed glass that had

once been the front doors, he saw Sparks' intention. He reached out and grabbed her, dragging her inside the burning building before she could run past it.

Their footsteps were amplified by the hardwood flooring in the building's foyer. A thick cloud of grey smoke collected along the ceiling, dulling the glow of the lights above them. However, it did nothing to hide the dead bodies scattered throughout the place. At least fifty corpses of various creatures, it undoubtedly provided a sample of what lay ahead in the city.

While fighting against the twisting and thrashing Sparks, Seb crouched down and leaned his back against a wall. He pulled Sparks down with him. To help her calm down, he whispered, "I won't let you burn. I won't let any of us burn. This is our only chance."

The last one in, Bruke dropped down so he couldn't be seen through the shattered windows and pressed himself against the wall beneath one of them. His mouth stretched wide as he fought for breath.

A millisecond later, the sound created by the rush of insanity came at them through the spaces where the windows had once been.

Because Seb couldn't see outside, he looked around the space they'd hidden in. The foyer had been ripped apart. Anything made from upholstery—the chairs, the tablecloths, the curtains—had been shredded. Deep gouges scarred the white walls. Bodies lay scattered across the hardwood floor. Blood of all different colours painted every surface.

Creature after creature then flashed past the smashed front doors. A constant stream, they spilled out into the desert. They had one thought on their minds: get to the source of the explosion.

Despite the thick smoke in the foyer and the creatures

tearing past outside, they'd made it. They'd gotten in without being seen. Seb continued to hold onto Sparks, who shook in his arms. He whispered to her, "It's okay. We're safe now." He looked across at SA to see her clip the leveller back to her belt. They wouldn't need it. Not yet anyway.

CHAPTER 17

The others gathered around Seb in the foyer. He wiped his stinging eyes—the smoke sending tears streaming down his cheeks—and continued to keep his voice low. "If we wait here too long, those creatures in the desert will be on their way back. I don't think it'll take them long to realise we're nowhere near the wreck."

The stomp of something large then ran past a smashed window next to them, shaking the ground with every step. So huge, Seb only saw a hip pass the windows.

When they could no longer feel the beast's steps, Bruke said, "But if we go too soon, we'll run into the stragglers."

"Exactly," Seb said. The looks from the others placed the decision squarely on his shoulders—again. Either option could land them in a whole heap of shit. They would stand by him, but he needed to make the choice.

A look around the foyer at the dead creatures and devastation, Seb then looked at Sparks. Although she returned his stare, her eyes flitted between him and the stairwell to the higher floors. Smoke poured through the gap beneath the door, flooding their space with a thicker and thicker cloud.

"Too much longer," she said, "and we'll pass out from smoke inhalation."

It had also grown hotter in the foyer from the fire above pressing down on them. Seb rubbed his burning eyes again, sweat as well as smoke making them sting.

Because nothing other than the giant had run past the windows, Seb nodded his assertion. He then showed his friends the palm of his right hand to encourage them to stay put, and moved in the direction of the hotel's exit. As he weaved through the bodies littering the hardwood floor, he did his best to avoid the many pools of blood like he had when he entered the place. They varied in size, consistency, and colour.

Now close to the doors and farther away from the roaring fire, Seb heard the shrieks of the beings out in the desert. A mob of wild animals in the still night, they howled their insanity at Kajan's permanent moon. Although indecipherable, something about their cries suggested frustration at the killings denied to them because of the abandoned wreck. It showed they had some basic form of cognition. Maybe enough to pull together into a hunting pack and flush the Shadow Order out of their city.

The air fresher near the exit, Seb breathed into his tight lungs. Just before he stepped out of the building to get a clear look, a small creature no higher than his shin appeared in front of him. An ugly little thing, it had long spindly legs and arms, green slimy skin like a frog, and a wide mouth filled with needle-like teeth. Its overbite made it look like a novelty bottle opener. As it looked up at Seb through its squiffy eyes, its jaw fell limp with a slight *clop.*

The creature then pulled in a deep breath to let loose a scream, but Seb darted forwards and stamped on it before it could. The rotund little thing burst like an atomic bomb, exploding with a shockwave that nearly threw Seb to the ground. The fierce release of air rushed through the hotel's foyer, momentarily clearing it of smoke. It shattered the few windows that remained intact, damn near turning the panes to dust as it thrust the glass out into the street.

His hands clasped to his ears, Seb opened and closed his mouth as if it would help relieve the ring in his skull. The small creature's innards had made a mess of his boot and the wall, painting them both with a thick green slime.

Even over his ringing ears, Seb noticed the absence of noise in the desert much like he'd noticed the absence of noise in the city when their ship blew up. A moment later, the creatures' cries lit up the night again. They were heading back.

Seb looked at his friends to see all of them staring at him with the same slack expression. He beckoned them towards him and shouted, "Quick, let's get the hell out of here."

While he waited for them—everything in slow motion—his legs buzzed with the need to run.

The second they left the foyer, Seb looked out into the desert and saw the shadows coming to life.

"Damn," Reyes said as the darkness turned into a mess of insanity. Creatures of all different shapes and sizes, they came forward in a line stretching so wide Seb couldn't view them all without turning his head from side to side.

Sparks turned to run into the city first. By the time Seb had spun around too, he saw she'd already stopped. More creatures were coming at them, a group of stragglers still emerging from the brightly lit streets. Only twenty or so. Not many if they had to fight them on their own, but they'd slow them down enough for the pack behind to catch up.

Because he knew Sparks wouldn't come, Seb grabbed her

and dragged her back into the hotel's foyer. She fought against him, twisting to get free from his grip.

"We can't go out there," Seb said.

"Where do we go, then?"

"Up."

While looking at the smoking door, Sparks shook her head. "No way."

Not a decision he made lightly, but certainly one he had to make quickly, Seb scooped Sparks up and ran for the door through the cloying smoke. Although she kicked and twitched in his grip, nothing would stop him from saving her life.

When he reached it, Seb grabbed the handle on the stairwell door and instantly let go. Too hot to hold, he stood on one leg instead and kicked it down with his suspended foot. He fell forward as it opened.

They rushed in as thick black smoke fell out, flooding the foyer. At least it would assault their pursuers too.

SA overtook Seb at the bottom of the stairs and led the charge, running into the darkness with Reyes and Bruke behind her. Seb put Sparks down. She dug her heels in again, her hands on her hips as she refused to move.

"Please trust me," Seb said. "This is our best option. Believe me, I didn't want to go underwater when we had to, but I recognised it as the only choice. I'll make this work, I promise."

The screams of the creatures outside now closer than before, Sparks looked back in the direction of the sound before pulling in a deep breath and running into the smoky stairwell after the others.

As Seb listened to his friends run away from him, he noticed a fire axe close to the door. A metal-handled tool, he ripped it free and wedged it between the door handles, the wooden floor shaking from the footfalls of the creatures that had entered the hotel.

Just as Seb slid it into place, he jumped backwards as something collided into the other side of the doors, forcing them inwards by a few inches. But the axe held.

The doors came forward with another shove, sending Seb back a second step before he spun on his heel and ran up the stairs after his friends. Despite the promise he'd made to Sparks, he didn't know what they were running into. But he did know it had to be better than facing what was gathering in the hotel's foyer.

CHAPTER 18

With only the sound of his team's footsteps to follow through the dense black smoke, Seb blinked against his stinging eyes and ran blind. He dragged his left hand against the wall to keep his bearings. An inhale to call ahead, it filled his lungs with the acrid, plastic burn around him. Stars punched through his vision as he coughed, every breath dragging more of the toxic air into his lungs.

By the time Seb stumbled past the fourth floor, the smoke had thinned a little. It still rose up the stairwell, turning the tall structure into a chimney, but the worst of the flames and smoke came from the second floor. That wouldn't be the case for much longer. The stairwell would soon be full.

Every breath relieved Seb that little bit more, and the sound of his friends speeding off ahead of him lifted his heart. If they were getting quicker, then he would too.

The ripping sound of tearing wood and then the clang of metal hitting concrete told Seb the creatures below had beaten his barricade. An instant later, the swell of insanity filled the tall cavernous space, their cries riding up on the back of the thick smoke.

It sounded like thousands of them below. Nothing else for it, Seb gritted his teeth and pushed through the lactic burn in his legs. So many different beings behind, some of them must be able to run through the smoke quicker than he could.

Six floors up, Seb quickened his pace and took the steps two at a time. Still thick with smoke, but it was better than lower down. Sweat poured from his brow into his stinging eyes, which he blinked against repeatedly.

The stairs shook from the weight of the beings on Seb's tail. Their loud calls made it harder to hear his friends ahead. But when he focused, he managed to tune in to them. They were still climbing.

The sign on the wall had a number ten on it in what must have been twenty different languages. The first one Seb had seen through the black clouds. The pack on his tail were gaining. Those in the lead were clearly through the worst of it. The echo of his own gasps taunted him; did he have it in him to go all the way, or would the creatures catch him on the stairs?

Smoke and sweat still stung Seb's eyes and partially blinded him. His own fatigue got fed back to him with the slaps of his heavy steps against the metal stairs. He spoke to his friends through SA. *How much farther?*

Reyes' voice came back. *Floor fifteen is the top. We've propped the doors open to let some of the smoke out.*

As Seb passed eleven, he pushed the sounds behind him to the back of his mind and ground his jaw against his fatigue. *I'll be with you soon. They're close.*

We're ready for them, Reyes said back.

At floor thirteen Seb heard the heavy slathering breaths of the beasts. Although he looked behind, he still couldn't see them. The ones at the front sounded like they moved on four legs rather than two. They were eating up the stairs as they ascended at a gallop.

A wobble kicked through Seb's legs, and he nearly fell. The strength had left him. He wouldn't make it. When he turned with the staircase to run up to the next floor, he saw it behind him. Somewhere between a wolf and a crocodile, the thing had a long forked tongue and a large mouth loaded with teeth. The sight of it gave him the extra burst of speed he needed.

Just as Seb started the climb to the fifteenth floor, a green blast flew past him and into the creature's face. It yelped before falling backwards down the stairs, its thick tail curling beneath it and turning it into a leathery bowling ball. The thud of it bounced off the metal steps on its way down.

At floor fifteen, Seb saw Bruke, SA, and Reyes. SA and Reyes were at the front, their guns raised and pointing down the stairs. Bruke had his gun and what must have been Sparks' weapon ready to hand over to them. He also kept the double doors propped open.

SA and Reyes parted for Seb, letting him through to the top floor before sending another barrage of fire down the stairs. The smoke meant they had to shoot blind. Screams of fury rather than pain responded to their attack.

Bruke tugged on Seb's weapon as he ran through. "Give me your gun."

As Seb handed it to him, Bruke explained, "I'm getting ready to swap their blasters around when they overheat."

At that moment, Reyes threw her automatic weapon down behind her. The light on the top of it glowed red. A second later, SA did the same. Bruke had already given a fresh one to Reyes, who fired down the stairs again. He then loaded up SA. Barely a pause in their attack, the two soldiers kept the advancing horde at bay.

"We'll stay here while you and Sparks find the best way out," Bruke said. He wiped his face against his shoulder. His eyes were red from the smoke, and he squinted as if he struggled to see through them. "We should be able to hold them back, but we don't know for how long."

No time for a conversation, Seb simply patted his thickset friend's hard shoulder as he passed him and ran onto the fifteenth floor to meet a furious Sparks.

Before Seb could say anything, Sparks pointed a long finger at him. "Don't you *dare* pick me up like that again. I'm not a child."

Seb pulled in a deep breath of the fresher air and looked at the doors on either side of the hallway. Just two rooms up there, it must have been the penthouse suites. The first door he tried didn't budge. Made from thick hardwood, he balled his fist and punched the thing from its hinges. A mess of splinters and wood dust, it revealed the room beyond. It had several sets of stepladders dotted around the place and cans of paint everywhere. "They must have been decorating when Enigma's call went out."

Although Sparks had followed him in, she ignored him. A bulge in her cheek from where she ran her tongue around the inside of her mouth as if it helped contain her vitriol, she took in the room.

The sound of automatic fire rang out from the stairwell behind them. They had time, but not too much. It wouldn't be long before either the smoke or the creatures got them. Seb needed to come up with a plan. He ran to the large window on the other side of the room. It overlooked the desert. The cold contact of his forehead touching the glass, he looked down at the ground. It gave him a view of the beings running in through the hotel's entrance. The line of creatures looked like it had no end. "This isn't the right room," he said.

"Maybe you should call reception and ask them to switch you."

But Seb ignored her, running back out of the room and knocking down the door that led to the suite opposite. A similar state to the first one, it had cans of paint and stepladders dotted around it. As he ran, he picked up a large tin of white emulsion and launched it at the window in front of him. It shattered the pane with a loud splash as it sailed through the glass and disappeared into the darkness outside.

By the time Seb got to the smashed window—the air considerably fresher—he watched the can of paint pop on the ground below. It left a large white explosion on the dark road. What would the fall do to a body? He shook his head to banish the image. This suite faced the city. To look down showed him a clear street. All the creatures were too busy running in through the foyer and stairwell.

Bruke's voice came at them. "Hurry up, Seb, they're gaining ground here."

"The buildings opposite are too far away," Sparks said.

Instead of replying to her, Seb ran back out into the hallway. He thought he'd seen it on the way through, but he couldn't be sure. When he got to the thick red fire hose, he grabbed the end of it and tugged, snapping it free of the plastic catch holding it in place. It unravelled as he dragged it away. Hopefully it would unravel far enough.

Seb ran back towards the smashed window, picking up another heavy paint can on the way through. The cool outside air rushed in as he closed down on it.

A decorator's grubby towel covered in paint lay on the floor by the window. Seb tied it around the handle of the paint can and then around the end of the hose. Although Sparks watched him the entire time, he didn't try to explain. Instead, he tossed the can from the window and watched it drag the hose out with it. The whoosh of the thick hose rushed over the window frame.

As the hose unwound, Seb felt Sparks stare at him while he watched it. When it snapped taut, he looked out of the window. The can of paint swung from where it hadn't quite reached the ground.

Sparks poked her head out next to him. "It's a couple of storeys short."

"We'll have to jump."

"A couple of storeys to you is very different than a couple of storeys to me."

"I'll send SA down first; she can catch you at the bottom."

"What is this? Toss the short person?"

"We could play burn the short person instead."

When Sparks didn't answer, Seb ran back out into the hallway and said to SA, *I'll relieve you. I need you to go and see Sparks. She'll tell you the plan.*

The second Seb reached the stairwell, SA threw her gun at him and ran back in the direction he'd just come from. He stepped forward, the gun pressed into his shoulder, and opened fire into the dense pack of bodies trying to get up to them.

CHAPTER 19

Seb remained at the top of the stairwell, his hands aching from the recoil of his gun. Sweating as much as ever, he blinked repeatedly, but it did very little against the sharp burn in his eyes. Tears ran down his cheeks while pains streaked up both sides of his face from where he clamped his jaw with the effort of the continuous offensive. But at least every shot landed; hard to miss because of the dense press of bodies. A massacre, but he had no choice. If he didn't kill them, they'd kill him.

The screams of agony and fury mixed together so loud it made Seb's head spin—that and the lack of oxygen, the smoke getting thicker with every passing second.

It felt like an age had passed before Seb finally heard SA. *We're down. The road's clear. Come now.*

The light on the top of Seb's blaster had turned from green to orange. After swapping weapons with Bruke, he paused for a moment. Loyal to the team, Bruke would have stayed there for as long as they needed him to. But one of them had to go next. "Leave the guns, and we'll hold them off until you're down."

Although Bruke looked like he wanted to argue, good sense must have told him not to waste any more time. He stood up, nodded as he moved the two weapons closer to Seb and Reyes, and ran out of there in the direction of the hosepipe hanging through the smashed window.

The second Bruke left them, Seb heard it. A deep baseline growl, it shook the walls and his vision. Although he kept firing blind into the thick smoke, he looked at Reyes. Before he said anything, SA came through to them. *What the hell was that?*

I'm guessing the giant we saw run past the hotel earlier, Reyes said.

Damn. Hurry up, Bruke, Seb said. The metal stairs then shook beneath his feet from what must have been the monster's ascent. He continued to fire, a deep ache balling in his shoulders from his weapon's recoil.

Reyes paused to swap guns. In the brief moment where she didn't attack, several small creatures like the one Seb had stamped on burst from the thick cloud. The world still in slow motion, he picked them off one at a time, each one exploding when he shot them. *Boom. Boom. Boom.* The blasts of air from each one drove the hair back from his forehead, dried the sweat on his face, and cleared the smoke momentarily. Then Seb saw the last one, its little mouth opened wide as it readied to bite him. It came to within a metre of him before he burst it with laser fire. Another loud *boom,* the foul little thing's sticky innards coated his gun, face, and hands.

Reyes returned to Seb's side with her gun, and for the next minute or so, they saw the faces and bodies of some creatures as more of them made it through the black smoke. They'd capitalised on Reyes' slight pause in fire, closing the gap between them. All different shapes and sizes, thankfully none of them were impervious to laser blasts—at least none of the ones they'd encountered so far. For someone who didn't have slow motion like Seb did, Reyes picked them off with a deadly accuracy better than him.

Is everything okay? SA asked.

A glance at the light on his gun, Seb watched the orange turn to burnt orange. *We're alive,* he said. The creatures now driven back into the smoke, they continued to release their shrill calls of pain as he fired where he couldn't see. The thud of the giant continued to climb the stairs. If it stamped down too hard, it felt like the entire staircase would collapse.

Slow motion on his side, Seb spun around, switched weapons, and fired into the darkness again. He'd managed to move quickly enough to keep them pinned back in the acrid smoke. At least, he hoped he'd kept them back; it was quite possible the smoke had thickened, reducing their vision and only making it seem like they were winning. The taste of burned rubber on the back of his throat had gotten worse.

Another loud roar boomed up the stairwell at them. The vibration of it nearly took Seb's feet from beneath him, and he stopped shooting. When he looked at Reyes, he quickly kicked back into gear. *How the hell are we going to take that thing down?*

Sweat glistened on Reyes' face, and veins stood out on her neck. She clenched her teeth as she shook with the blaster's rapid fire. Although the others would have heard him, Reyes responded, *We can only deal with it when we see it. I'm hoping the answer will be obvious then.*

Another switch of her gun, Reyes spun back around, and they continued to stave off the attack. The thud of footsteps continued to climb the stairs, a slow, torturous progression amidst the chaos. It told them nothing could stop it.

SA, Seb said, speaking so everyone could hear, *where's Bruke?*

We haven't seen him yet.

Seb and Reyes stared at one another before returning to the fight. *WHAT?*

He hasn't appeared.

BRUKE! What the hell? We need to get out of here. Where are you?

"Here."

Both Seb and Reyes looked behind them to see Bruke. He panted from the effort of rolling the large metal barrel he had in front of him. He'd flipped it on its side. It had white linen stuffed into one end.

Easier to talk through SA despite their close proximity, Seb said, *What are you doing?*

Still struggling for breath, Bruke said, *Stand back.*

Although Seb and Reyes moved back towards Bruke, they continued to fire down into the stairwell. The creatures continued to vocalise their agony and rage as their shots landed.

When the giant roared again, Seb noticed Bruke jump and nearly send the barrel down the stairs too early. It took for him to step closer still before he smelled it. *Where did you get the fuel from?*

Don't tell me you're starting MORE fires? Sparks said.

As much as Seb wanted to ignore her, he knew her fear. *You're down there. This won't come anywhere near you.*

His breathing back under control, Bruke pointed toward the two penthouse suites. *They have a generator up here. I drained it of fuel. I also found the rest of their supply.*

Three more barrels were lined up in the hallway, all of them had white linen poking from their tops like giant Molotov cocktails. Next to them, Seb saw a large red metal can.

I also found this. Bruke held up a lighter for Seb to see.

The light on the top of Seb's gun had turned orange again from him continuing to shoot. *My gun's about to run out, Bruke. Are you ready to send it down now?*

By way of response, Bruke put the lighter's flame to the white linen. It caught, and fire engulfed it within seconds. *Stand back.*

Although aware of Bruke's actions, Seb focused on swapping his gun around again. He looked up in time to watch the flaming barrel bounce down the stairs into the smoky abyss.

More screams than before, it clearly hit some of the creatures on the way down. And then it stopped, glowing in the smoke.

Another deep roar, closer than ever, and Seb watched the barrel get stamped out, the fuel igniting for a second before it got completely smothered. The vibration of the giant's foot shook the entire hotel.

Are you okay? SA said.

Fine. Reyes looked at Seb and Bruke before returning to where she'd been standing and firing down into the darkness again. *For now.*

Before Seb could return to her side, Bruke had another barrel on fire and rolled it down after the first. He sent a third one straight after it.

The orange glow of the flames came to an abrupt halt about four metres below them as it hit what must have been the wall of creatures they were holding back. Seb watched the fire swell as all the barrels burned together. Too much for one giant to stamp out. *Send the last one down. We need that fire as big as we can make it. Hopefully it'll give us a chance to get the hell out of here.*

Both Reyes and Seb stopped shooting and moved out of Bruke's way for him to send the final barrel down after the first three. It crashed into the others, the flames reaching higher than ever. The giant yelled. From the way the flames danced and weaved, it looked like the creature was trying to bat them out, with little success. Its voice rang much higher in pitch than it had a few seconds ago.

Reyes then ran off into one of the nearby rooms. She came back a moment later, shoving an armchair in front of her. When she got to the top of the stairs, she grunted from the effort of lifting it before she lobbed it down. It disappeared from sight, an uneven roll sending out thuds as it hit random stairs on its awkward descent. It smashed into the flaming barrels, momentarily disturbing the hypnotic orange sway.

Seb smiled in spite of their situation. *Reyes, you're a genius!* He and Bruke took off at the same time and ran to the rooms to get more furniture to build their bonfire.

CHAPTER 20

Holding the last piece of furniture he could find, Seb yelled out as he threw it down the stairs into the burning barricade. A coffee table, this time it rolled no farther than a metre before it hit the stack of backed-up furniture. At least a flight of stairs deep, only the side of the pile closest to the creatures burned. He allowed himself the briefest moment to watch the flames before nodding. *That should hold them.*

Reyes stepped beside him and looked down. *I think you might have spoken too soon.*

Despite their clear screams of pain, Seb watched as the creatures grabbed the burning furniture, lifted them to their tipping point against the railings, and then sent them down the gap in the centre of the staircase. An armchair chased the headboard of a bed to the ground, smacking against the metal barricades all the way down, aggravating the creatures climbing up.

Bruke, Seb said, the thick smoke damn near blinding him despite him shielding his eyes with his forearm, *is there any more petrol in that can? We need to light the rest of the furniture while we still have the chance.*

Although he didn't reply, Bruke darted into the hallway before rushing back in with the red fuel can in his hand. He undid the lid as he ran, discarding it on the metal stairs with a *ting*. He then doused the fire before saying, *Get back.*

Both Seb and Reyes stepped away as they watched Bruke swing the still-open can backwards before launching it onto the pile. For the briefest of seconds, the can disappeared into the smoke.

Has he missed it? Reyes said.

Whoom! The petrol caught, lighting the stairwell brighter than Seb had seen it so far. The fierce rush of heat shoved them back.

Seb covered his eyes again as he backed away several more steps into the hallway. When he pulled his arm down, he stared at where they'd come from.

Bruke? Seb said. Before he could say anything else, the thickset creature appeared.

Seb ran forward and checked him for burns. *Are you okay?*

Bruke nodded.

Now he knew his friend was okay, Seb peered into the smoking and fiery mess. He couldn't see anything, yet he still knew the truth of it. *They have more bodies than the fire can burn. Their sheer numbers will win out sooner or later. We have to block the doors too.*

Before either Reyes or Bruke could respond, Seb ran back into one of the rooms and straight over to a window. He jumped up, gripped the long curtain rail above it, and yanked it down as he landed. They needed as many as they could get, so he ran to the next window and did the same. A quick glance at the door showed him Reyes sticking her head in before she ran into the room opposite.

All the poles from the one room in his arms, Seb ran back

to the double doors, dropped them on the floor with a clattering splash, and picked up just one. He slid it through the handles. *Bruke,* he then said, *come here.*

The lizard creature came to his side, and Seb nodded at the curtain pole. *Can you bend that around the handles?*

Impatience in her voice, Sparks said, *What are you guys doing up there?*

Setting fire to shit, Seb said as he watched Bruke bend the metal pole. He picked up the next one for him and slid it through the handles like he had with the first. *Now stay hidden, stay quiet, and only come out when you see us coming.*

CHAPTER 21

Every time Seb or Reyes slipped a curtain pole through the door handles, Bruke bent and tied the metal like he would a rope. By the time they'd done the last one, Seb shook his head at his friend. He laughed in spite of their situation. *You're a beast.*

A slight sagging of his shoulders, Bruke whined.
Not in that sense. Like a beast-mode beast.
And that's good?

A loud roar in the stairwell was followed by the thud of more falling furniture. Seb batted his hand through the air to end their conversation. *Doesn't matter. Get down the hose now.*

Although Bruke looked like he wanted to argue about who went first, it only took for Seb to scowl at him before he turned his back and ran to the room with the smashed window.

A few seconds of silence between Seb and Reyes, they watched where the hose was attached to the wall. It pulled taut when Bruke started his descent. Reyes kept her eyes on it as she said, "Who's next?"

"You. Then me."

Like Bruke had, she looked like she wanted to argue, so Seb cut her off. "That's an order, soldier."

A deep inhale and sigh, she nodded. "I'll wait by the window so I can go the second he's jumped off." A moment's pause, she then hugged Seb. "Good luck, and don't do anything stupid."

As Seb stood in the hallway—smoke squeezing through the gaps in the doors—he felt more alone than he had in a long time. The creatures' fury, and now their pain, had rung shrill for so long he shut it out as no more than background noise. Then he heard it again. The *thud*, *thud*, *thud* of more falling furniture. He already knew it, but in case he'd forgotten, the creatures' desire to get to him and the others burned stronger than the flames holding them back. Bruke and Reyes had better be quick.

CHAPTER 22

How are you doing, Reyes? Seb asked her.

About halfway down. Bruke's safe too. We'll be ready for you shortly.

Seb had already stepped several paces towards the hotel room with the smashed window. With a tight grip on his blaster, he watched the double doors leading to the stairwell through unblinking and stinging eyes. The thuds on the other side beat with more frequency. The beasts were dumping the furniture quicker than ever. No doubt some of the creatures down there were impervious to fire. Maybe they'd found their way to the flaming blockade by now and were helping out.

Then Seb heard it. A high-pitched scream, the thing sounded much closer than any before. He watched the double doors. At least one of the creatures had made it to the other side. It sounded small, but how long would it take for its larger mates to catch up?

Seb took another backwards step into the room with the smashed window.

Another loud thud of more falling furniture.

The doors moved. It looked like a testing push. They

slowly opened inwards. The metal poles had enough slack for the gap between them to stretch by an inch before they resisted. The second shove snapped forwards in a clear sign of the creature's impatience.

Then what must have been a body slam hit the other side of the doors. They snapped forward again. Seb raised the butt of his blaster to his shoulder and looked down the barrel. *Reyes, speak to me.*

Is everything okay? Reyes said.

How are you doing?

Bang! The doors snapped forward again with even more force. The poles still held, but the gap stretched wider than before. Something much larger had made it to the top. It roared, more smoke coming through the gap in the doors. A slight tightening of his trigger finger, he heard Reyes finally reply, *Nearly there.*

Bang!

Seb jumped back.

Bang! This time he heard the sound of ripping wood. The poles might hold, but the doors were going to get torn from their hinges before long. Another step backwards into the room, his heart racing, his already dry throat turning drier still.

Now! As Reyes said it, the doors tore free. Still tied together with the poles, they slapped down against the floor. A gargantuan creature with thick black skin, red eyes, and a long blue tongue fell through on the back of them. But it hadn't always been black-skinned. From the pink cracks all over its torso, Seb saw it was the giant that had chased them up the stairs. The one whose hip he'd seen pass the window of the hotel foyer. From the state of it, he guessed it must have been burning for the entire time. It looked up, fixing Seb with its glare. Its red eyes glowed brighter as if it knew it would get its revenge.

Seb turned and broke into a run at the smashed window. *They're through.*

A slight slack on the hosepipe, he grabbed it as he ran and let it slide through his hands.

The sound of smaller feet and the stampeding run of the giant chased after him.

No time to look back, Seb reached the open window, jumped up onto the ledge, and kicked off, thrusting himself out into the cold night.

A world in slow motion, Seb's palms burned from the friction of the hosepipe as it sped through his grip while he fell.

CHAPTER 23

A slow-motion view of things, Seb tried to take his focus away from the burning pain in his palms. The friction bit into them. It felt like it was tearing his skin off. But he gripped on tighter. Better to be palmless than dead.

Above him, Seb noticed one, two, three, and then the giant burst from the broken window he'd just leaped from. Their desire to get to him had clouded their judgement. Their faces showed the dawning realisation too late. They clearly hadn't seen the hosepipe in his hands. They'd clearly forgotten they couldn't fly.

All four creatures caught up to Seb as he fell. Until that point he'd doubted the hose slowed him down. He squeezed tighter.

One of the creatures looked like a gargoyle. Short, squat, and heavy. It had tiny wings, which it beat with a ferocious intent. They must have been for decoration because they did nothing to help the ugly thing.

The giant's mouth hung open as a cavernous hole. It roared fury at Seb, throwing a long charred arm in his direction as it passed him. The tip of its fingers caught him and sent him swinging, but he managed to hold on.

At least seven storeys from the ground, Seb finally came to a halt. The cool air around him gave some relief from the scorching hotel and his burning palms. He looked down in time to see each of the creatures hit the ground with a *thump*. The planet seemed to shake when the giant connected. Four dead bodies, they'd landed on the spilled white paint as if they were projectiles aimed at a target. But none of them had split like he'd expected them to. They all lay inert, and he saw blood seeping from the giant's still-open mouth. No matter how aggressive they'd been towards him, none of them deserved to die.

Screams above Seb took his attention. From the hotel's penthouse suite, he saw tens of faces peering down the hosepipe at him. One of the creatures tugged on it, which shook him a little, but not enough to make a difference.

The growls and grimaces fixed on him, Seb remained in the same spot and connected with Sparks. *Sparks, I need you to keep an eye on them on your computer. I'm hoping they'll all be drawn to the window to watch me rather than work out they need to come back down the stairs.*

Sparks' voice came back to him. *No problem. From what I can see, they're still on their way up at the moment. Oh, wait ...*

Seb jumped, her sudden change making his heart kick. *What?*

You need to hurry.

She didn't need to say anything more. Seb let his grip loosen a little, sliding with a control he certainly hadn't had when he'd first leaped from the window.

The hose shook again. Their efforts were as ineffective as

before. At least that was what Seb thought. Until he looked up.

They're trying to cut you down, Bruke said.

One of the creatures at the front of the pack had pulled a shard of glass from the shattered window. The bright glow from the city glinted off the impromptu blade. Even with the distance between them, Seb saw the beast's teeth from its determined grimace.

Still six storeys from safety, Seb looked at the window in front of him. On his way up, the smoke had been thinner on the higher floors. That looked to have changed. No matter how hard he squinted, he couldn't see through the room for the black churning mess of smoke in there. He couldn't risk going back in.

Sparks came through again. *They're coming down the stairs. It looks like those at the bottom haven't yet worked out why, but it's only a matter of time. As soon as they realise where we are, they'll be on us in seconds.*

Seb loosened his grip and slid quicker than before. The hose continued to shake, and although he put distance between him and the creatures above, he saw more of the beasts were copying the actions of the first. Several glinting shards were now gripped by several busy hands.

Five storeys to go. Seb looked over his shoulder at his friends below. They all stood on the white splash of paint, waiting for him.

The hose snapped with a *crack!*

Still in slow motion, Seb watched the beings above him as he fell backwards. The top half of the hose leaned over him, pulling him away from the building. Several of the beasts hung out of the window to look down at him.

Go limp. SA's voice.

Even with his world slowed down, Seb didn't have time

to question it. He put his trust in his love and focused on relaxing his body. The wind from his fall buffeted his ears.

A second later, Seb hit the resistance of his friends. Although not much time to process things, he had enough awareness in slow motion to feel all of them bend their legs to cushion his fall. A hard shockwave snap ran through his body, but nothing more. Much better than hitting the solid ground.

Reyes and SA helped Seb stand up. SA then wrapped a tight hug around him. *I'm so glad you're okay.* She pulled back, took him in with her bioluminescence, and kissed his lips before Sparks pulled her away.

The main pack are on the third floor. Those in the foyer are going to get the hint soon. We need to go now.

A second longer than he should have taken, Seb smiled at his love before he followed the small Sparks away from there.

CHAPTER 24

⨳

The friction burns on Seb's palms stung. He opened and closed his hands as he ran, but it offered little relief. Although, now in the light of the city, he'd had a chance to look at them, and they weren't anywhere near as damaged as he'd expected.

Like when they'd run from the desert towards the burning hotel, the group moved at Bruke's pace. At least it gave Sparks plenty of time to look at her map and guide them out of there. The insanity behind them grew slightly quieter with their progress, but nowhere near quiet enough.

As Seb darted around another mutilated corpse, his stomach tightened at the stench. A putrid acid tang of the beast's spilled guts, it took all he had not to vomit while he ran. Another advantage of their pace, it made it easier to avoid the many body parts waiting to trip them up. Bad enough to bear witness to the aftermath, at least he hadn't been on Kajan to see the slaughter.

Seb saw what looked like the same revulsion he felt on the faces of his friends. *How many beings have died here, Sparks?*

There used to be a population of around fifty thousand in the city. From a few cursory scans, I'd say there are five thousand left at the most. I'm not sure how many made it out into the desert, but I don't think we need to worry about them.

Even at Bruke's pace, Seb couldn't avoid the glistening pools of blood and soft innards. He winced at the squelches and splashes underfoot. A shake of his head, he spoke as much to himself as he did the others. *The sooner we get off this planet, the better.*

They were now several blocks away from the hotel. Each and every building threw a neon assault at them. Despite being in amongst the garish glow, Seb's eyes still hadn't grown used to it. It didn't help that they hadn't yet recovered from the smoky stairwell. He continued to open and close his hands even though he doubted it did anything for his sore palms.

The distressed cries from the creatures behind had dimmed a little more. That was something at least, but Sparks said the creatures on the higher floors of the hotel had worked out they needed to come to ground again. Surely it wouldn't be long before the pack caught up to them.

Reyes must have had the same thought because she looked behind while she ran. *We need to move quicker.*

As the leader, Seb needed to make the unpopular decisions. *We move as a team.*

An unusually spiteful reply, Sparks said, "Then we fall as a team." Her voice bounced off the walls around them.

It took a few seconds for Sparks to look at Seb. When she did, shame ran a hard wince through her features. *No one gets left behind,* Seb said.

Tears ran down Bruke's face, and he shook his head. *Please go without me.* His mouth spread wide as he gasped from the effort of their run. *I'll find somewhere to hide.*

No, Sparks said. *I'm sorry, Bruke. I'm scared is all.*

We all are, Seb said. *But we need a better plan than just running. They'll catch up to us soon.* As if on cue, the sounds of footsteps called to them from a few streets back. After looking behind—the others doing the same—he added, *Very soon.*

Sparks turned her computer around several times as if orientating the device would somehow make their route clearer. Anxiety spiked adrenaline through Seb's gut to watch it. *Do you have any idea where to take us?*

At the head of the pack, Sparks led them down another street. On the other roads, the dead bodies had been on the ground as dark lumps, but this street had been used for prostitution. Tighter than the others, it had as many dead bodies on the ground, but it also had windows lining each side. Red lights shone through each one. Only about one in ten had their curtains closed. The other nine showed them the extent of Enigma's wrath. Brightly lit booths, the brutalised bodies of every creature he could imagine and more. Many of them were lucky if they'd remained in one piece. Even then, they didn't look to have gone painlessly: slit throats, slashed stomachs, dismemberment, decapitation ...

A look at his friends, Seb saw all of them—save for Sparks, who had her attention on her screen—look at the dead creatures. They must have had a hard life while they lived, and then they had to be on the receiving end of this. The taste of bile in his throat, he tried to level his breaths while he ran. He couldn't overthink it. Not yet. Not now.

The only safe place to look, Seb stared over Sparks' shoulder at her screen. *I don't care if you don't know where we're going, but please get us off this street.*

Although Sparks didn't reply, Seb saw her effort to do what he'd asked of her in her deep frown. He had to trust her guidance. Apart from missing the rocks on their landing, she'd never let him down before.

The footsteps behind them had grown louder. The calls of the beasts in the pack swelled through the streets they'd just run down.

Sparks suddenly threw a sharp left. The first truly dark alley they'd come across, Seb stopped at the entrance to let the others through first. As a gasping Bruke took up the rear, he looked back the way they'd come from. Bodies on the ground and in the windows. Red everywhere from the lights to the spilled blood. The sound of the creatures behind them gathering momentum. The now familiar insanity created by Enigma.

They're close, Seb said to the others after following Bruke into the darkness. About to push Sparks again for some kind of plan, he watched the small Thrystian stop by what looked to be a hatch to a cellar. A metal doorway, it leaned at an angle, showing it led down into a basement of some sort. A padlock kept it shut, which she shot with an electric bolt from her computer.

While the others helped Sparks pull the heavy doors open, Seb divided his time between watching them and looking back the way they'd come from. The creatures would be on them soon.

The creak of the metal doors' hinges yawned through the alley as SA, Sparks, and Reyes all opened them and laid them down gently. Sparks ran in first, her torch on her computer out in front of her. Bruke, Reyes, and SA followed behind. Seb bounced on the spot as he watched them before he finally darted in.

The mocking groan of the old hinges cackled as they closed the doors again.

Just as the second door came to rest—the bright glare

outside getting cut off—Seb heard the beasts enter the alley. He stepped away from the doors and raised his blaster, the others around him doing the same. The cavernous space amplified their heavy breaths, and when he looked to his left and right, he saw his gun wasn't the only one shaking. *If nothing else, this narrow space will slow them down like the stairwell did. Hopefully that'll be enough for us to hold them back.*

The vibration from the creatures' stampede made the doors hum in their frame. Seb stepped forward to pull on them to keep them quiet, but Reyes grabbed his arm. *It's an ambient sound. They won't notice it.*

Remaining where he stood, Seb stared at the doors as if they'd provide some kind of insight about their chances of survival. Although dampened because of the barrier between them, the noises of the beasts' lust to obliterate sounded no less intense.

The swell of creatures grew thicker. Seb hooked his tense finger over his trigger, cramps running through it as he fought his desire to squeeze.

When a thud hit the doors, it took everything Seb had to keep his head, but the beasts continued to sail past. Another thud, the doors lifted from their frame, a splash of light flooding in before they clattered back home again.

For the next five minutes, they listened to the crowd thin to silence.

Sparks finally turned her torch from the metal doors to the darkness behind them.

Seb saw the others look with him into the gloom. *Where are we?*

In the tunnels.

The what now?

Kajan has always had an undesirable aspect to it. In its

more conservative past, they had to be a lot more covert. The gambling and prostitution took place underground rather than on the streets. There's a network of tunnels that the authorities never knew about. Or if they did, they turned a blind eye to them. They used these to move from one establishment to another. It was a gamble, but I thought if we could get into these, it might help us avoid the creatures chasing us. I can't see any beings down here on my scanners, so I'm hoping it will lead us straight to the monument SA saw.

And Seb saw—not that he wanted to share that information.

A scratching sound then came at them from the darkness. Seb lifted his rifle again, those around him doing the same.

When Sparks raised the torch on her computer, it lit up a line of creatures. The light caught the glint in their eyes. Another sweep and it picked up the wink of their blades. Armed with both knives and swords, they were clearly ready to use them.

After letting go of a hard sigh, Reyes said, "So much for it being abandoned."

CHAPTER 25

Her mouth hanging slightly open, Sparks looked from her screen to the creatures in front of her and back to her screen. As Seb watched her repeat the gesture several times, his upper body locked tight against his desire to pull his blaster's trigger. Slight changes in posture on either side of him showed him the others had a similar reaction. They were so tuned in to one another, they'd all slightly adjusted because of Sparks' clear shock. They were all ready to fight on her say-so.

Sparks finally spoke while pointing at her computer. "I can see you on my radar now. Why couldn't I a minute ago?"

Before any of the strangers had a chance to respond, Reyes moved quicker than Seb had ever seen her travel. On her way through, she grabbed Sparks' computer, finishing in front of the largest of all the creatures, Sparks' torch and the barrel of her gun pointing in its face.

The being looked to be their leader. A good head and shoulders above the others, it stood about eight feet tall. A muscular body covered in hair, it had small arms and large powerful legs. Its tail—as thick as a python—flicked a couple of times. Because he didn't know what the gesture meant, Seb watched it in case it went for Reyes. Although the creature didn't step back, it winced away from the glare in its eyes.

In the tense silence that followed, Seb and the others raised their guns and stepped forward. Reyes had made the call, so they had to back her up. Let her take the lead. The creatures in front of them all lifted their blades. They looked confident in the way they carried them, like they could hold their own against blaster fire. Maybe they knew something Seb and his friends didn't.

The creature at the end of Reyes' scrutiny moved slowly, letting its knife drop to the ground with a *cling* and raising its hands in the air. Although its voice shook, a certain menace laced its deep tone. "We mean you no harm. We're in the tunnels to escape what's going on up there. I'm guessing that's what's driven you down here too?"

Reyes shone the torch from one of the beings to the next, each one squinting in reaction to her scrutiny. A mismatch of creatures, they ranged in height, build, and species. The bright interrogation seemed to be enough for her, and she relaxed her stance.

What's going on, Reyes? Seb said. *This isn't a hostile situation. Unless you have a* very *good reason, please don't turn it into one.*

A dip of her head at their leader, Reyes backed away, speaking to the ground. "I'm sorry. I mistook you for a different species."

What the hell was that about? Seb said.

Ice clung to Reyes' reply, and her eyes narrowed to slits when she glared at him. *Just move on, yeah?*

As long as you promise not to do that again. We've made it this far, it would be good to stay alive to get to Enigma.

I said just move on.

After he'd looked at the perplexed expressions of the rest of the team, Sparks shrugging to show she had no idea either, Seb let it go. He trusted Reyes with his life. Whatever her reasons, he'd know them soon enough. Just not now. He turned his attention to the line of beings in front of them. "Can you lead us to the Pillar of Peace in the main square?"

Their leader didn't respond for a few seconds. It finally spoke, answering the question Sparks had asked them rather than Seb's. "There are a lot of us down here." A look at Sparks' computer, the large creature continued, "The reason you didn't pick us up is because these tunnels are lined with zinconium. It makes us invisible to scanners. It helped the criminal underworld stay hidden in the old days. Maybe we're being paranoid thinking the crazies above can use any tech in their current state, but we're staying deep in the tunnels just in case. Before we go any farther, we need to know, can we trust you?"

Seb noticed the slight flick of the creature's eyes to Reyes. He stepped between them and nodded. "You can. I promise what just happened won't happen again, will it, Reyes?"

The marine shook her head. Whatever had driven her to confront these creatures had passed.

With a gentle nod, the tall leader said, "Why do you need to get to the Pillar of Peace?"

After a moment's pause, Seb looked at his friends again. Too much information could give this creature power over them. "We don't know yet."

"Huh?"

"The chaos above has been triggered by something. We think the pillar has played some part in that. We plan to turn the slaves back to what they were before this."

"Slaves?"

"It's only the slaves who have turned."

"Why?"

SA came through to Seb. *Only tell them what you have to.*

Silence swept through the place. Both sides gave off the impression of standing at ease, but the slightest spark between them would turn the dark tunnel into a bloodbath.

"We're from the Shadow Order," Seb went on. "You may not have heard of us, but we're your best hope of stopping the craziness above."

After a look at the creatures on either side of it, the tall and hairy brute relaxed its stance. "We'll take you to where you need to go."

Seb lowered his blaster so it hung by his side. His team did the same. A nod, he watched the leader for any hint of insincerity. Always hard to tell with a species he hadn't met before, but he couldn't see any. "Thank you."

As they set off into the darkness of the tunnels, the creatures in front of them lit their way with torches. The bright glare of the combined glow glinted off the metal-lined walls. It must have been the zinconium the creature had talked about. Sparks and Reyes beside him, he noticed Sparks snatch her computer back from Reyes while scowling at her. Her back tense, she looked one step away from hissing at the marine.

Although he'd lowered his gun and the creatures in front of them seemed legitimate, Seb still said to the others, *I think we're going to be all right, but keep your wits. I don't trust them.*

CHAPTER 26

I'll be glad when this is all over.

Seb looked around to gauge the reaction of the others to SA's comment. They all peered ahead into the darkness, following the creatures and their torches. Even if she had spoken to the rest of them, he chose to keep his response private. *Me too. I'm tired.*

So much has happened in such a short time.

A nod, Seb continued to look around at the metal-lined walls. A uniformity to them, it reminded him of the Shadow Order's base. Like when Moses led him around the place, their current guides could be taking them anywhere. *Hopefully this will all end with the fall of Enigma. I feel like we've had a lifetime's worth of shit happen to us in just a few months.*

The slightest of glances his way, SA said, *I never thought I'd say this, but I feel ready to settle down. I want to live a slower-paced life. I thought I'd be a soldier for a long time. You've changed that ... I suppose that's what love does to you.*

Robbed of a response, Seb reached across to her. She took

his outstretched hand and squeezed it. Maybe he should have told her then that he'd also seen a vision of the pillar, but he didn't understand it yet. He knew there to be more to it, and until he'd wrapped his head around what that was, he needed to keep it to himself.

Their guides stopped in front of them and pointed down a dark tunnel that looked much like all of the others. Every time one of them moved their torch, the light sparkled off the zinconium-lined walls, floor, and ceiling. It made it much harder for Seb to keep his focus on their guides. Then he saw what they were showing them. A few metres along, the metal-lined walls gave way to concrete. The second they stepped out there, they'd become visible to scanners again.

The hairy, thick-tailed leader said, "That's the way to the Pillar of Peace. There's a hatch up ahead. Go through it and you'll be in an alley that runs directly to the square."

Before Seb could thank them, Sparks looked up from her computer. "Why did you take us the long way?"

Aware of Reyes in his peripheral vision, Seb saw the twitch in her form. Because he had slow motion on his side, it gave him the time to dart across and stop her mid run. He caught her before she reached their guides and shoved her back, wrapping a tight grip around her upper body as he restrained her. "What's gotten into you?"

"I don't trust them." Her raised voice echoed down the tunnel.

Seb made eye contact with Bruke and flicked his head to call him over. "I need you to restrain her. We'll need her if we fight, but I'm still not convinced these creatures mean us any harm. And, Reyes, keep your voice down, yeah?"

Once Bruke had taken Reyes' gun from her grip and clipped it to his side, he wrapped his two strong arms around the feisty marine so Seb could step away.

One last glance at her to be sure she'd at least calmed down enough to remain restrained, Seb turned to their guides. "I'm sorry. I don't know what's gotten into her." He threw another glare in her direction.

With a gracious nod, the large hairy brute spoke with a soft tone. "We're living in tense times."

"That we are. Although"—Seb rested one hand on his gun at his hip—"I don't mean any disrespect, but I have to insist you answer Sparks' question. Why take us the long way?"

Only subtle, but with so much reflected light in the space, Seb couldn't help but notice the glint on the creatures' blades from where they all held them. Sparks and SA must have seen it too, because when he turned to them, he saw the small Thrystian had her blaster raised to her shoulder, and SA had drawn her knives. Bruke continued to hold Reyes back; in her current state, she might end up their most effective weapon, but they could only let her go as a last resort.

The tall leader stepped closer to Seb. It kept a tight grip on its knife. "I told you we have our loved ones down here with us."

Seb waited for it to continue.

"Just like we're strangers to you, you are to us. We don't know you, and we don't want to put those most dear to us in danger. We took you the long way around to bypass them. We've put our trust in you; I would ask you do the same."

Maybe Reyes' reaction had given him the jitters because Seb couldn't think straight. SA clearly sensed that. She came through to him. *It seems legit.*

While shuffling on the spot, the leader of their guides said, "We plan to stay put. If you plan to be on your way, we don't have any reason to fall out."

Because none of the others offered anything to him, Seb looked at their guides, their frames more tense than they had been at any other time since they'd met them. "If you'll stand aside and let us pass, we'll be on our way."

The leader looked at Reyes.

"We'll keep her restrained until we're away from you. Tell them, Reyes, you won't come back here." Then so his team could hear, *Don't put us in the line of fire because these things have triggered something in you. We don't see the same threat you do, so you need to trust us.*

One of their guides shone their torch on Reyes. A mix of rage and grief swam in the glow of her brown eyes. She growled at it through clenched teeth. "Get that thing out of my face before I ram it up your—"

"Reyes! Wind your neck in." Since they'd accepted her into their team, Seb had only seen Reyes as an equal. It felt awkward to pull rank on her, but she'd been in the military, so he had to use her Pavlovian response to an order to keep her in line.

Her reluctance to obey clear in her tight jaw, Reyes looked up and down the line of creatures. "It's the wish of my team that we move on. I don't trust you, and if I were on my own, I would have cut every one of your throats and left you to bleed out on your zinconium floor."

Three of their guides raised their blades in her direction.

A pause to look from one to the other, she said, "*But*, you have my word that I won't come back once we've passed. I won't betray my team like that. That's worth a lot more to me than anything."

To watch her complicate their situation lifted Seb's body temperature, and he tugged on his collar. He looked at the lead creature, who flicked its head to the side as an order for its team to move over. They shuffled closer to one wall. The three who'd drawn their blades kept them drawn.

Bruke took the lead and dragged Reyes past, the feisty marine glaring at them the entire time.

While Sparks and SA followed, Seb bowed at the tall leader. "Please accept my sincerest apologies. I'm not sure what's gotten into her. She's normally one of the most level-headed beings I know."

"Tense times," the lead guide said, repeating its sentiment from earlier.

"That it is. Thank you for guiding us, and know we'll do everything we can to put a stop to the insanity up on the streets."

The guides watched Seb, but none of them spoke. They were clearly impatient to get rid of them.

As hard as he found it to not look back, Seb walked away from them, giving them his trust as he focused on his team up ahead. The small glow of Sparks' torch looked pitiful compared to the combined glare of what had led them there. But other than losing their torchlight, he felt glad to be away from the creatures.

CHAPTER 27

Just in case any of them looked back, Seb waited until they walked around the bend in the tunnel before he said, *Sparks, are they following us?*

No. They might not have remained where they were, but they definitely haven't stepped out of the zinconium.

Seb then turned to Reyes. *What the hell were you playing at? You nearly got us into a fight we didn't need to have. What's wrong with you? Have you not killed enough beings yet?*

Although Bruke had let go of Reyes, he remained close so he could grab her again should he need to. A scowl at Seb, she said, *It doesn't matter. It won't happen again.*

I think it does matter. If you need trigger warnings, I'd like to know. Then it hit him. *It's something to do with the Faradis, isn't it?*

Reyes spun around with her gun raised and pointed it at Seb. Despite Bruke's close proximity, SA got to Reyes first and pressed the tip of one of her knives to her throat.

Even in the darkness, Seb saw the marine gulp and then lower her weapon. The point of SA's knife forced her to keep her chin raised. Tears swelled in her eyes before running down her cheeks. A few tense seconds before she said, *I'm sorry. You're right, it's all to do with what happened on the* Faradis. *But now isn't the time to talk about it, so please don't mention it again.*

Seb reached out to SA and tugged her back. Although reluctant, SA lowered her knife and stared at Reyes as she stepped away. *I've had no reason to doubt you until now,* Seb said. *I get that whatever happened on the* Faradis *has left a lasting impression, but please remember we're in this together. We're here for you, but don't drag us down with your past trauma.*

I'm sorry. It won't happen again. For real this time. I'm sorry. While Reyes spoke, tears ran down her face. A tough woman, her expression remained stoic despite her clear show of emotion.

Come on, Seb said. *Let's get out of here and find that damned pillar.*

CHAPTER 28

The bright neon glow of the city dazzled Seb as he stepped from the tunnel and held the cold metal doors open for the others to follow. Although he looked up and down the alley, blinking repeatedly as if it would somehow help him clear his vision, he could only see a wash of brightness.

After a few seconds, Seb's sight returned. By then, all of the others had already stepped out into the open. Because Sparks' computer had told them the way was clear, he'd had to trust that.

As the last one out, SA helped Seb close the hatch behind them. The hinges creaked like the ones on the doors at the other end of the tunnel, although they protested with slightly less enthusiasm. Too quiet for any being beyond the alley to hear.

Now his vision had returned, Seb glanced up at the permanent night sky and shivered. It must be miserable to live in such a cold and dark place, and with the light pollution amped up to the max, the residents would have to leave the city to get a view of the stars. Such beauty taken away from them by retina-scorching advertising and the always open brothels, casinos, and hotels. Although, what else could they do in such a wretched place other than gamble and fuck?

The others had been waiting for Seb, but it took for him to look at them again to realise that. *Sorry, I got a bit lost in my thoughts.*

While pointing up the alley with one of her long and bony fingers, Sparks said, *The main square and the pillar are that way.*

With a nod, Seb set off, passing through the middle of his friends so he could lead the way. None of the others seemed willing to take up the role. *No time like the present. Let's get this over with and then hopefully find our way off this cursed planet.*

Although Seb strode ahead, Sparks ran a couple of paces to catch up with him and walked at his side. They avoided the scatterings of mutilated bodies by either going around or stepping over them. The tight space made it comfortable for just those two, the others bringing up the rear.

Seb felt Sparks looking at him, but he kept his focus on the square ahead while he spoke to her. *What do you think the pillar will tell us?*

The glow of her screen added another light to his surroundings. *I'm not sure,* she said. *I just hope we find whatever it is quickly. There doesn't look to be any organisation to the chaos running around the city, which I think makes it much harder to deal with.*

How so?

It's hard to predict when they'll find us again. It could take days, or it could take minutes. What I know for sure is it's just a matter of time. Hopefully, we can find out what we need to and be out of here before our luck runs out.

At least the square's clear, Seb said, but before he could step out into it, Sparks grabbed his arm in a tight grip, her long fingers clamping around his bicep. Were it not for the panic in the way she clutched onto him, he might have yelled out at the sharp pain. Instead, he stifled his response and let her drag him back a few steps. As he focused on Sparks, he felt the others watching them.

Several taps against her screen, Sparks then turned it around to show Seb eight blue dots out in the square.

Huh?

Stealth armour, she said, glancing at the others before she tilted the screen so they could see it. *They're wearing stealth armour. I can only guess they're doing that to remain invisible to the slaves so they don't get attacked.*

SA pointed at the mini computer. *You think they're protecting the pillar?*

I'm certain of it.

That's something at least. When the others looked at Seb, he elaborated, *We must be on the right track if the thing's being guarded.*

Bruke wore his usual frown of anxiety and shrugged. *So what do we do? How do we fight something we can't see?*

Silence followed as they all watched Sparks work on her computer. She manipulated the map, pulling it back to give them a wider view of Kajan. It showed the cluster of red dots that were the thousands of enraged slaves. *They're not close enough to be a problem,* she said.

Yet, Reyes said.

After nodding her small head, Sparks agreed. *Yet. As soon as we go out in that square, the noise of the fight will draw them straight to us.*

After a look at his friends, none of them offering anything useful, Seb returned his attention to Sparks. *So what do we do?*

Although she didn't speak, Sparks brought up a screen on her tablet that made no sense to him. A mess of lines, it looked like a complex network of cables all running their own path to somewhere he couldn't see. Her fingers blurred as they flew across the screen's surface. He heard it before she said anything: a deep bass boom coming from what sounded to be monstrous speakers. It was far away.

Sparks pulled her map up again so they could see the cluster of red dots. They were running towards the noise. *They have a flagship casino that hosts a lot of events. Fights, concerts, sports matches ... I've just turned the sound system up full. It should buy us some time.* When she brought her screen back to the square, she showed them the blue dots hadn't moved. *They must have strict instructions to stay put.*

Seb still couldn't see a way around their problem. *So the slaves won't bother us for a while, but that doesn't suddenly make those guards visible.*

Sparks, Reyes said, *can you orchestrate the battle from the alley? We can't see the guards, but you can tell us where they are if we go out there.*

Seb joined the others in staring at Reyes. When she looked back at them, she raised her eyebrows. *Unless you have any better ideas?*

Nothing.

Reyes pointed out into the square. *If we pretend we can't see them, I reckon we could go out there and walk down another alley. We could get them to follow us. Once we've drawn them out of position and lured them into a tighter space, we could open fire. We can make the environment work for us.*

Bruke this time: *You think that'll work?*

It's the best I've got, Reyes said.

The others looked at Seb. He thought about it for a second before nodding. *It's the best we've got.*

CHAPTER 29

Where the change from the dark tunnels to the brighter alley had momentarily blinded Seb, the square looked like it would do the same. It raised the brilliant glare another notch, and just peering into it made his eyes sting. Hopefully he wouldn't fall over any of the scores of dead bodies littering the ground. Just before he stepped out with Reyes by his side, he looked back at Sparks. It took a second for her to lift her attention from her screen. *You ready?*

No.

Do you need more time?

I need a better idea.

Butterflies did backflips in Seb's stomach as he stared at her. *Really?*

Sparks then batted him away with a wave of her long hand. *Just get on with it, yeah? I know this is the best plan we've got. Wishing it wasn't won't change that. I'll do my best.*

It took for Reyes to shove Seb out into the square to kick-start him into action. She quickened her pace to catch up with him, and they fell into stride, staring straight ahead at the alley they were heading for.

Vulnerable in the glow of the main plaza, Seb imagined the eight guards watching them and resisted the urge to look across at the Pillar of Peace. If they blew their cover, they'd be filled with holes in seconds. Instead, he divided his attention between where they were heading and the ground, the finer details of the corpses' mutilation hidden to him because of the dazzling lights around them.

The disco Sparks had started sounded louder in the open space. A baseline boom called through the city. It unsettled the beat of Seb's hammering heart. It sounded like the monotone thud could go on forever; hopefully it would hold the slaves for as long as they needed it to.

They'd agreed they'd only speak if absolutely necessary. Sparks needed to have control of their communication. She came through to them, her tone soft as she clearly tried to help them keep their heads. *They're moving towards you slowly. I can't be certain, but judging by their gradual approach, I'd say they still think they have the advantage. I don't think you should stay out in the open for too long. All it will take is for one of those eight to lose their head and open fire. Just stick with the plan and you might have a chance of making it out of here.*

The closest alley still a couple of metres away, Seb did his best to centre himself as he walked. It probably looked unnatural for him and Reyes to be silent, so he said, "How are we going to get out of here?" Before Reyes could reply, he added, *Just say anything. I want the guards to think we don't know they're there.*

"I'm not sure. Not with all those lunatics running through the streets. Do you think we can find a ship somewhere?" A wooden performance at best, hopefully the guards' lack of familiarity with Reyes made it sound passable.

Sparks came through again. *They're following you a little bit quicker than before. I think they can see you're going to disappear from sight any second now. Keep it up.*

The desire to run sent a series of twitches streaking through Seb's legs. They dared him to break into a sprint. A deep breath, he focused on moving at a slow pace. Unable to resist looking at the Pillar of Peace, he turned in the direction of the milky-green jade monument. Although Sparks had described it to him, he couldn't appreciate its magnificence. At least three metres tall, it stood in the middle of the square. Because it was lit up from every side, it had four shadows.

They've stopped, Sparks said. *They must think you've seen them.*

"No matter how many times I see the Pillar, I can't even get over how beautiful it is," Seb said, fighting to keep the warble from his voice. A look up its long and thick shaft, he added, "I'm not sure I could even name all the religious symbols on there."

Less successful than Seb had been, Reyes' voice shook as she played the game. "I'm not sure any of those religions are about now. You know what this galaxy's like for fads and how quickly they change. I would guess the majority of them are defunct."

The end of Reyes' words echoed in the alley as they stepped into it. The shadow created by the close walls helped Seb relax ever so slightly. Anything had to be better than the spotlight glow of the square.

Reyes threw a quick glance at Seb, her eyebrows raised. *I suppose this is it, then?*

Before he could reply, Sparks said, *They've sped up; they're following you in.*

Seb rested his palm against the cold metal handle of his blaster. It took all he had to not turn around and face them. *How many?*

Five.

And the other three?

Staying by the pillar. I'll count you down from three. Three ...

A quickening of his pulse, Seb drew a breath to bring his world into slow motion.

Two ...

Because Seb didn't know if the creatures could see them yet or not, he refrained from looking at Reyes.

One.

Seb and Reyes spun around and opened fire. Both of them released a barrage of green blasts, the shadowy alley lit up by their rapid assault. Although he knew the guards to be there, it still looked strange to see the blasts halt when they hit solid air.

What must have been thirty to forty shots hit the invisible wall in front of them. The second Seb saw one of his blasts fly out into the square beyond, he lowered his aim and watched them sink into something on the ground.

Sparks then said, *Stop! They're all down. Their dots have gone off.*

Seb rode his quickened breaths and watched SA and Bruke emerge from the alley opposite. Although Sparks' voice came through to him, he knew it to be directed at them.

About one metre to the left of the monument.

Despite having a blaster on her hip, SA threw just one knife.

Seb ran to the end of the alley to see if it hit its target.

By the time Seb stepped out into the square—standing on the pile of dead guards as he passed over them—he saw the knife SA had thrown. He jumped when she sent a series of shots into the downed guard. Now she'd tagged it, she had to make sure she finished it.

A pool of blood at his feet, Seb stepped away from the guards they'd killed and heard Sparks again.

The last two are coming right at you, Bruke, she said. Seb watched Bruke open fire, spraying blasts out in front of him and spinning on the spot as he did so.

When a line of green laser fire came his way, Seb jumped back over the dead guards and into the alley he'd just stepped from. *Bloody hell, Bruke!*

Turn left, Bruke, Sparks said.

He turned right.

The other *left.*

He turned right some more.

As much as Seb wanted to help, friendly fire pinned him and Reyes in the alley. *Bruke, what are you playing at?*

But he didn't reply. He'd clearly lost his head.

Sparks then shrieked, *Help!*

The shrill call rang through Seb's skull. He looked across the square to see she'd been lifted from the ground and was being carried away.

As the closest, Bruke ran into the alley after her. At least it stopped him shooting. The slowest in the group, he found a burst of speed before he jumped over the top of the small Thrystian and spread his arms wide.

It did the job, Sparks falling from having been dropped. But the two guards grabbed Bruke instead, lifting him from his feet.

Before Sparks could open fire, a force field exploded to life between her and the invisible guards. She shot it all the same, her blasts ineffective against the yellow-tinged barrier.

Bruke yelled, "Help!"

Seb, Reyes, and SA ran across the square to join Sparks. They all opened fire on the force field. It remained strong against their onslaught, and Bruke vanished from their sight.

The panic of the past few minutes had left Seb breathless. Pains streaked through his tight chest. He panted as he said, *Bruke, we'll find you. Just tell us where you're going.*

It's too late, Bruke said.

What?

At that moment, an engine started up and the whooshing sound of a booster flew through the streets so loudly it drowned out the baseline from the casino. A ship then thrust into the sky at a forty-five-degree angle, an orange tail of flame behind it. It glowed like a comet against the night.

Don't worry, Bruke, we'll find you.

Bruke didn't respond.

Seb looked at Sparks. "Where are they taking him?"

While shaking her head, Sparks kept her focus on her tablet. "I don't know. They've got something on that ship that's stopping me tracking it. I don't think he can hear us either."

Reyes leaned over her and looked at the tablet. "Zinconium?"

"That's my guess."

Seb dragged his hair back from his forehead. "Then how are we supposed to find him?"

The sound of the casino pounded through the streets, louder because of the silence from his friends.

CHAPTER 30

The silence only lasted for a few seconds, but it felt like much longer, even with Seb allowing for his current slow-motion view. Sparks finally broke it. "My guess is that Enigma have taken him."

The four of them huddled in the dark alley. They watched the force field that had prevented them from saving their friend vanish as if it had never been there. Seb shrugged. "So we continue with our plan and hopefully find Enigma and then Bruke through that?"

Sparks' eyebrows rose in the middle, and she winced an apology. "It's the best I've got."

As he let go of a sigh, Seb's entire body sagged. "Too many plans are the best we've got rather than the best plan." Before Sparks could defend herself, he raised a halting hand at her. "That's not a criticism, just an observation." When he looked at the others, none of them offered anything better. "I'd say it's the best any of us have." Both SA and Reyes dropped their focus to the ground as if to confirm his assertion.

As their leader, Seb needed to keep them moving. "We

can't give up hope for Bruke's safety," he said. "Sparks is right, nothing's changed. We still need to find Enigma and, hopefully, that means we'll find him too."

Only a slight lift in those around him, but slight had to be better than none. They had something they could hang on to, a path to follow. They had to keep moving forward, and Seb had to lead them. "Is the square clear, Sparks? We've definitely killed all the guards?"

It took for that moment for Seb to see the tears in Sparks' eyes. She pulled her glasses off to wipe them before she put them back on again and flicked through several screens on her computer. "Yep, we're good to go."

"And how far away are the slaves?"

"They're still in the casino."

The sound of the place continued to call through the city. It had been there all along, but with everything else going on, Seb had stopped hearing it for a time. Because none of the others moved, he led the way back out into the brightly lit square. He ran towards the Pillar of Peace at a jog. The seemingly levitating knife in the downed guard helped him see where the body lay so he didn't trip over it.

Seb stopped in front of the tall obelisk and looked all the way up its shaft. He pressed his hand to its cold surface and felt one of the many carved images. The shape looked to be the representation of a badger. No idea what sect it belonged to and what they thought about the galaxy, but at least they'd chosen a cool animal to represent them.

His palm resting against the jade, Seb felt a throbbing pulse run through it. Similar to when he healed people, except it came from the stone into him rather than the other way around.

The others appeared at his side, looking the pillar up and

down like he had. Their confused frowns suggested they were at a loss for ideas too.

SA shrugged. *I'm not sure why I got a vision of this. I don't know what it means.* When she looked at Seb, he turned away. She must know he'd seen it too.

Sparks stepped closer to the monument and picked at it with one of her long fingers. A chip of jade came free and fell to the ground. Seb winced as if he felt the stone's pain. Despite not having any affiliation to any of the religions represented, they were damaging a sacred monument—probably the only sacred object in the secular city of sin.

It took for Sparks to shine her torch into the hole before Seb saw the different stone inside. It sparkled like a diamond. A red grid replaced the torch's beam coming from Sparks' computer. It scanned the stone beneath the layer of jade.

When Sparks pulled away, her attention dropped to her computer as she clearly assessed the results of the scan. Seb pressed the tip of his finger against the translucent and sparkling stone. The second he made contact with it, a rush of images overwhelmed him. A planet covered in the same crystal he currently touched, it had a sprawling palace made from the mineral. It looked like it had grown from the ground rather than been built. On the roof of the place, he saw a lady who looked to be in her sixties. She had white hair that rested against her long flowing robes of the same colour. Her eyes were brilliant green. She looked like an angel, but something about the sight of her twisted anxiety through him. For a moment, he watched her without her knowing, but then she stared straight at him. The radiance of her glare dealt him a physical blow. He gasped and stumbled away from the obelisk.

Two steps back, Seb tripped over the invisible body of the dead guard and landed on his bottom, the hard ground running a skeleton-jarring shock up his spine. As he looked up at the other three, he saw all of them staring down at him, waiting for an explanation. He only had one word. Sparks said it at the same time as him. "Varna."

Sparks must have gotten the hint that Seb had nothing more to say. Distrust aimed at him, she then looked back down at her computer and read from the screen. "Varna is where this mineral comes from." She looked back at Seb. "How did you know about it?"

"Just carry on, yeah?" Whatever he'd seen, he couldn't and didn't want to explain it. Although he felt SA focus on him with the other two, he refused to look at her, his cheeks burning. She already knew he'd had a vision that he hadn't shared with her.

Sparks continued. "The mineral's called stalt. It's worthless, but it's been long believed that it can be used for psychic broadcasts. Like an antenna sends out radio waves, stalt does the same for psychic ones. It must have been why the guards were here. They clearly didn't want anyone getting too close to the pillar. Had Bruke not shot everything but the guards, there wouldn't have been a chip in the jade and we wouldn't have found it." After a moment's pause in the wake of her mentioning Bruke, she said, "Varna's not far from here. As a planet, it's pretty dead. At least, that's how it looks from the surface."

The palace and the woman with the green eyes burst into Seb's mind.

Reyes looked between Seb and Sparks. "You think it's Enigma's base?"

"It has to be," Sparks said. "They need stalt, and that's where it is. Most of the planet is made from it. It's the best place to send their commands from. It's such a worthless planet I didn't think of it before now."

A sharp nod, Reyes stood taller than she had since Bruke vanished. "That's where we need to go, then!"

But we don't have a ship, SA said.

Her attention back on her computer, Sparks didn't reply. Instead, she tapped furiously at her screen.

Only a background noise, but when the music in the distant casino stopped, all four of them looked in the direction of it.

"What's happening, Sparks?" Seb said, the stillness of the planet almost deafening.

She didn't look up from her screen, her fingers moving over it quicker than ever. "I'm not sure. There's no reason why the power would go out there and nowhere else. Either the slaves have worked out how to shut the place down, or …"

"*Or?*" Reyes said.

"Enigma have done it."

Reyes threw her arms up in a shrug. "Why would they shut the casino down?"

A shrill alarm then rang through the city. High in pitch, it called out loud and clear. The slaves in the casino screamed in response to it as if answering the call.

The sudden change in their circumstances sent a surge of adrenaline through Seb that forced him to his feet. "I think that answers our question."

"Both of them," Sparks said. "That sound's coming from the closest ship to this square. That's our ride out of here." She paused as if listening to the screaming slaves before she added, "Now we need to get to it before they do."

CHAPTER 31

The glare from their surroundings made it impossible for Seb to see Sparks' computer screen. He adjusted his stance, moving slightly to the right. It helped, but how did Kajan's residents ever get used to it? How were they not blind after spending a few months here? Since he'd been in the city, the lights burned his eyes and his face ached from squinting. Now he could see better, he watched Sparks draw a line with her long finger. She traced from where they were in the square to the ship with the alarm going off.

Although Sparks talked, Seb barely heard her, his attention on the mass of red dots heading for the very same spot they wanted to get to. The alarm called to the slaves, who screamed back at it. "And there's no better option than that particular ship? There's not one farther away that's quieter?"

With a shake of her head, Sparks sighed. "Those guards knew what they were doing. All the other ships in this city are docked in the desert." Again, she used her finger to point at a spot on the map. The route to all of the other ships would take them straight through the pack of red dots. "I'm guessing that noisy ship was flown in after the chaos spread through the city. There's no way they would have been allowed in before. They've landed in the middle of a large road, blocking a main street."

A knife protruding from the being next to them, Reyes stared down at it for a second. "Why don't we just put their stealth suits on?"

"I thought about that," Sparks said, "but they have antennas in them."

Seb and the other two stared at her.

It took her a couple of seconds before she realised she hadn't told them enough. "Enigma can operate them remotely. They can turn them on and off at will."

"Like they can control the ship we're about to board?" Reyes said.

Sparks shook her head. "I can override that. I understand the tech in ships. I wouldn't have the first clue where to start with the nanochips in a stealth suit. I'm not even sure I'd be able to make it visible to work on in the first place, and certainly not in the time frame we have."

The mass of dots continued to close down on the ship. Before Seb could say anything, Sparks did. "If we're going to beat them to the ship, we need to move now. We'll be pushing it if we wait much longer. Come on."

Glad to follow his small friend, running helped Seb escape some of the anxiety ripping through him. Not that it was any consolation, but they moved much quicker with Bruke absent.

Sparks took the lead, with Seb behind her, and SA taking up the rear behind Reyes. They all followed the small Thrystian as she ducked down a nearby alley, dodging the dead bodies lying on the ground. Still brightly lit, but nothing compared to the stark glare of the main streets.

They turned left, right, and left again. In slow motion, Seb had time to look at Sparks' screen and the progress they made towards the ship. His ears told him they were drawing closer, the ship's alarm still calling through the city. The cries from the slaves continued to call back.

Because Seb had his attention divided between Sparks' screen and not tripping over the corpses everywhere, when Sparks stopped in front of him, he nearly went over the top of her.

A flash of irritation at Sparks' sudden halt, before Seb could say anything, he saw the reason for it. "Damn!"

One of the burning buildings had collapsed across the alley, leaving a landslide of bricks. Even if they could climb over the large and unstable pile of rubble, it burned with the fire that had clearly weakened its structure in the first place.

Sparks shoved Seb out of the way as she spun around, doubled back, and took another route.

At the back of the pack now, Seb watched Sparks take two more lefts to get them back in the direction of the ship. The sound of the slaves drew closer.

Sparks stopped again, and her shoulders sagged. "Shit."

A narrow alley, it was packed with several burning vehicles.

Her eyes wide, her words breathy, Reyes looked around them, scanning the windows of the nearby buildings as if they were being watched. "They've set us up. These look like they were dropped here by something."

Now he'd caught up to Sparks, Seb looked at her screen and gasped. Already out of breath, the sight of the red dots made it even harder to recover. The slaves were just a few streets away from the loud ship. No doubt their path had far fewer obstacles too. He spoke through SA. *I think we should hide out and get to the other ships. I think—*

The roar of a missile cut him off. When he looked up, he

saw it streak through the sky above them. Bright orange against the night, it ran in the direction of the casino. Even the sounds from the slaves stopped, as it had clearly captured their attention too. A second later, it landed with an almighty *boom!* A large orange explosion gave birth to a black mushroom cloud.

That's the rest of the ships gone, Sparks said.

While looking from the sky to Sparks' map, SA said, *I don't understand. Why wouldn't they just send the missile into the city to kill us?*

It took a lot for Sparks to lose her nerve, so when Seb watched her hands shaking as she typed on her screen, his stomach clenched. After a couple more taps, a swarm of about twenty blue dots appeared on her map. They moved as a group and they were heading their way.

Reyes stated the obvious. *They have more guards in stealth suits in the city. We're not going to make it to the ship in time.*

Although Sparks didn't speak, Seb saw her concentration as she glared at the map. Smarter than the rest of them, she looked to be formulating a plan. The blue dots were a street away from the red dots and two streets away from them. They were all homing in on the shrill alarm of the ship. Impatience got the better of him. *Come on, Sparks, you must have an idea.*

Sparks went to work on her computer.

Seconds later, the bright glare of the city blinked out. There were still glowing patches from the fires throughout the place, but otherwise they were in total darkness, the white pinpricks of the stars above suddenly visible in the vast sky. The slaves fell silent. The blue dots stopped moving.

Then the blue dots set off again, getting closer to the red ones. They must have seen the opportunity to pass them. The ship continued its synthesised wail, so close to them, yet so inaccessible. Instead of setting off towards it, Sparks continued to type on her tablet.

Her flurry ended with a definitive tap against the screen. The slaves screamed again, the sound lifting the hairs on the back of Seb's neck.

Sparks smiled at the others, the glow of her computer reflected in her glasses. *Enigma aren't the only ones who can influence those suits. I might not be able to prevent them controlling them, but I can control them too.*

Reyes said, *You just made them visible in front of the slaves?*

Yep. Hopefully it'll take Enigma a minute to react.

That's all well and good, Seb said, *but we still need to get past the slaves and the guards to get to the ship, and we can't see a damned thing.*

Sparks didn't let him finish before she set off again. He pushed his irritation down, balling his fists as he watched her head back the way they'd come from. Just before he could repeat their quandary—now running through an alley as dark as Enigma's soul—the Thrystian used her computer to project a red glowing schematic of what lay in front of them. She quickened her pace as she said, *We can see a lot more than they can.*

CHAPTER 32

One thing about following the red grid schematic was it masked the brutality of the massacre that had occurred on Kajan. The corpses were reduced to red-lined lumps, which Seb avoided while following the others.

When Sparks turned the schematic off and stopped, Seb and the others halted behind her. The street they were on stretched wide, although not as wide as the street they were heading for. The bright moon and the burning buildings lit their way.

I told you we'd get here, Sparks said.

As much as he wanted to be optimistic, Seb didn't have it in him at that moment. His pulse pounding, his chest tight from having inhaled more smoke while they ran, he also had a stitch working against his hopes of escape. *By here, you mean just about to step out into madness with the odds stacked squarely against us, right?*

With screams of rage just around the corner, they didn't need Sparks' map to see where the slaves were. Seb could hear them closing down on the ship fast, the shrill alarm drawing them in. Galloping feet hailed a mob of thousands on the move again. The run-in with Enigma's soldiers had slowed them for a minute at the most. As the sound of their charge came forward, it swelled through the main street in front of them like a raging torrent. Now they were close, it came down to who could run the fastest.

We'll be fine, Sparks said. *It's just like we've planned; follow my lead and we'll get out of here.*

Maybe she knew the response wouldn't be enthusiastic. Maybe she saw the futility of checking they were all okay with the plan. Not a good plan, but the only one they had—again. And it could work.

Sparks ran out onto the main road first. The second she broke away from cover, the slaves roared, the pace of their charge quickening.

Seb burst out behind her with Reyes and SA on either side of him. He dared not look back at the slaves. They were so close he heard their ragged breaths, their slathering need to destroy. When they yelled again, the sound crashed into him like a strong wave, and he nearly lost his legs. Their roars swelled to the point where he could have sworn the ground shook.

As Sparks ran towards the flashing ship, she pulled a grenade from her belt and tossed it behind her without looking. It sailed in an arc over them. On any other day, Seb would have watched it, but he kept his focus on the noisy vessel in front, his breaths quick, his legs burning as he sprinted.

A *bang* and bright spark exploded in a magnesium glare. Even with his back to it, Seb was dazzled, so it must have done something to the mob of slaves. While blinking away his blind spots, he kept moving at a flat-out sprint.

His vision back, the ship right in front of them, Seb looked over his shoulder. Sparks' flash bang had slowed the mob down. Not much more of a gap between them, but an increased gap nonetheless.

Sparks reached the ship first, jumping into the open back and running straight for the cockpit. Although SA reached it next, she hung out of the back doors and opened fire into the slaves running towards them. So numerous, she had no other choice but to spray her blasts in the hope of slowing down as many as possible. If she'd thought about using the leveller, she hadn't made it obvious. It would do so much damage it would hinder their chances of escape.

Seb arrived at the ship next, letting Reyes through before he pressed his blaster into his shoulder to help SA slow the chaos coming towards them. Or at least try to. His teeth clenched against the kick of his weapon; his trigger finger ached from where he clamped it so tightly.

The slaves fell to their blasts, but for every one they took down, twenty replaced them. *We've not got much time out here, Sparks.*

Nearly there, she said, *I need to break Enigma's control over this ship so they can't do anything to us in the air.*

Ten metres between them and the slaves, Seb looked at SA. A scowl of concentration, she continued to indiscriminately fire on them. *If we don't get out of this,* he said, *I want you to know—*

Shut up and keep firing.

The light on the top of Seb's gun had turned orange. It got darker by the second.

Then the ship's engine started, the loud roar of it replacing the shrill alarm.

As Reyes lifted them from the ground, SA and Seb continued to fire on the slaves.

Both of their weapons failed at the same time. Several

slaves took the opportunity and leapt at them, hanging onto the ship as it rose into the air.

Although SA kicked one off, two managed to get into the back with them. A world in slow motion, Seb saw the weak spot on the one he faced. Taller than him by a few inches, the creature had leathery skin covering its vulnerability on its chest. A hard jab, he drove the air from the creature and it stumbled backwards, falling from the ship, spinning over until it landed in the horde below.

The creature SA faced stood no taller than about three feet. After burying a knife in the top of its head with a wet squelch, she kicked the now limp thing out of the open back.

They shared a look with one another before Seb pressed the button to close the hatch. As he let go of an exhausted sigh and wiped sweat from his brow, he called towards the cockpit, "We're good to go."

The ship lurched forwards, picking up speed as it flew over the top of the dark city. The change from chaos to calm made Seb's head spin. He looked out of the back window at the fires burning in different places like candles at a vigil.

The built-up area behind them, Sparks shouted, "Bombs away!"

A click ran through the ship, which Seb felt as a vibration against the soles of his boots. He watched out through the back window as an explosion hit the desert's ground, swelling and rising up from the sandy plain. The shock of the blast sent them snaking left and right. While holding onto a handrail above him, he said, "What the hell was that?"

"A gift from Enigma," Sparks said. "It was rigged to blow if we got any higher than we are now."

Reyes then lifted their trajectory, pulling them up into the atmosphere and away from the cursed planet.

Seb sighed and met SA's bioluminescence. "It feels like

what we've just gotten away from should be a cause for celebration. But there was so much death and destruction down there. So much unnecessary carnage."

A moment's silence, Sparks called back to them, "Yeah, but look on the bright side: it's not like we have to go to Enigma's base or anything."

The words took what little strength Seb had left in his legs, and he slumped onto a bench opposite SA. After a second or two, he reached across and held both of her hands with his. In her eyes, he saw the same apprehension that gnawed away at him. What would they find on Varna?

CHAPTER 33

The gangway between Seb and SA was so narrow their legs touched. It allowed Seb to continue to hold her hands while resting back in his seat. He released a long sigh. When he looked up, he saw her watching him. *I can't believe what we've been through already. Yet it feels like we haven't even come close to facing the worst of it.*

A squeeze of his hands, SA tilted her head to one side in inquisition. *Who's to say this is going to be the worst of it? It might be a walk in the park.*

Enigma created *what we've just fought our way through. And now we're going to step into their base. I can't see it being anything but hellish.*

But they're hiding like snakes beneath a rock. Maybe that's a sign of how little strength they have.

That's true. But what if I can't do it?

Why does it have to be on you?

Because I'm supposed to be the chosen one. *What does that even mean? I'm not my ancestors. They could move moons and manipulate planets. What can I do? Slow time down and punch people. Act first and think later. Hardly the skill set of a hero, is it?*

SA leaned closer, her brilliant gaze fixed on him. *What you bring is greater than any magic trick your ancestors might have had. You're a leader. We're all here because of you.*

Although Seb opened his mouth to reply, SA cut him off. *Even when you can't do something, you've learned to trust in us to get it done. Sure, you've made mistakes; we all have. But you have integrity in everything you do. That's inspiring. That's why we follow you, and that's why I love you. We'll bring Enigma down as a team. One way or another.*

Unable to reply because of the lump in his throat, Seb felt the warmth of his love's hands squeeze that little bit tighter. He pulled in a deep breath, rested his head against the wall behind him, and closed his eyes.

CHAPTER 34

It felt like just seconds had passed when Seb woke to Sparks saying, "We're here."

He came to with a start, his heart surging. A similar reaction to when his alarm clock went off too early, his pulse galloped towards panic, and he felt like he couldn't breathe.

After a couple of seconds of blinking and rubbing his face, Seb looked at SA. She stared calm bioluminescence back at him, a gentle smile as she waited for him to level out. One final deep breath, he nodded, and both of them stood up at the same time.

Although he moved on weak legs, Seb stepped into the cockpit first, grabbing the headrest behind Sparks with both hands to keep him stable.

Aware of SA moving to stand behind Reyes, Seb stared out of the window and gasped. A vast desert of glimmering crystal stretched out below them. The same mineral they'd seen in the Pillar of Peace, it reflected the sun like a mirror. A structure rose up from it that sent his jaw south. A huge and ornate palace. The one he'd seen in his vision back on Kajan.

"Wow," Sparks said, her voice distant. "You can't see any

of this on the scanners. Enigma must have some kind of cloaking tech around the whole place. I'd normally be able to pick up a structure this large."

The sprawling palace must have had at least fifteen bedrooms. Dotted with tall spires that shot into the sky, they pointed up as sharp talons in defiance of the galaxy beyond.

For some reason, Seb's attention fell to one particular spire. Not the widest or tallest, but the most important of the lot. It had a large open space in front of it. Almost like a balcony but bigger than any he'd seen before. It looked like it probably had the best view of the planet around them. An image then punched into his mind, and he stumbled, his legs turning weak as he held himself up with the back of Sparks' seat. The same woman he'd seen when he'd touched the stalt in the Pillar of Peace: a slightly older woman with white hair and clothes; human, despite the green glow to her eyes. Maybe, like him, she simply looked human.

As the vision rescinded, Seb felt SA's hand on his back. Still rattled, he looked at his love as he tried to make sense of what he'd just seen.

You okay? SA said.

Seb nodded. What could he say to that?

Sparks then raised her computer, showing Seb the screen. A schematic of the palace. Although he could feel SA's attention on him, he continued to watch the small Thrystian's device while she spoke.

"At least now we're close, I can see where we need to go." She pointed to a room at the building's heart. It appeared to be a large hall. "Enigma are sending their broadcasts from this room here. I'm guessing they have some kind of technology that can harness the energy in the stalt on the planet. They must use the entire palace as a transmitter. We get in there and we're golden. At least, that's what I think anyway."

All the while Sparks spoke, Seb looked at the grand structure. It appeared to grow larger the closer they got to it. At first, he'd taken it to be mostly abandoned. A building like that should have an army out in front of it. Then he saw them. Only three creatures, they stepped from one of the many archways leading into the place. "I'm guessing there's more where they just came from?"

Sparks winced. "I was waiting to show you that." A tap on her screen filled the schematic with blue dots. Hundreds, if not thousands of them. Normal service resumed.

Tension gripped Seb's stomach, and his heart beat double time. As he let go of a long exhale, his cheeks puffed out. He finally found his words. "Is it too late to turn around?"

Instead of replying to him, Sparks said, "But look." She showed Seb a green dot on the screen.

Not sure what it meant, Seb simply stared at it. It certainly hadn't changed his mind.

"Bruke's inside," Sparks said. "I couldn't trace him from Kajan, but now we're close, I can see exactly where he is."

The first good news he'd heard in a while and the motivation he needed to push through his fierce trepidation. A nod to himself, Seb closed his eyes and filled his lungs, his entire frame lifting as he inhaled. When he reopened them, he saw more guards had come from the palace. Maybe thirty already, maybe more. Only a fraction of what Sparks had shown him. He reached across and squeezed Reyes' shoulder. "We've come here with a job to do. This is the final run, so let's get in and out as quickly as possible. Hit them with everything you've got, soldier."

CHAPTER 35

The entire ship shook when Reyes pulled the triggers on her flight sticks. Red lasers—several inches thick—flew away from them and rained down on the palace at the emerging guards. Bipeds and quadrupeds in all different shapes and sizes. They all fell, ripped apart by the brutal assault.

The blasts that didn't take down the creatures crashed into the palace and ground, sending showers of stalt crystals exploding away from their impact. To watch the place get torn apart lifted relief in Seb, and he almost smiled when he said, "Maybe we don't need to leave the ship to get Bruke out of there. We could just blow our way through."

More guards rushed out, and Reyes mowed them down. Insignificant compared to their firepower, the guards had no chance. A pack of them resembled large cats and were nimbler than the others. They avoided her first few shots, but even they fell in short order.

The ferocity of the continuous cannon fire shook Seb's vision. Some of the stalt—so completely obliterated—turned to white clouds of dust. In other places, the shattering palace sent a storm of dagger-like shards raining down on the guards.

While Reyes destroyed the place, Sparks worked on her computer. Not unusual for the screen to mean nothing to Seb, it took for Sparks to look at him with an ashen face before he realised they had a problem. "What?"

"They have another phase planned."

The noise of the battle rang out, and the ship shook more than before as the ever-increasing swarm of guards shot back. Their blasts did little against the ship's force field other than to wobble them in the sky and add to the chaotic sounds of war. Seb shouted so Sparks could hear him. "What are you talking about?"

Enigma have a three-phase plan, Sparks said.

Seb turned his hand over to encourage her to continue. *Go on.*

Phase one was to release chaos. Phase two was to pull the slaves together so they could wipe out the planets, like we saw on Kajan.

And phase three?

Total annihilation. They're going to wreck every planet. Reduce them to rubble so they can rebuild the galaxy in their image. They plan to take what's useful to them—like resources and tech—and destroy everything else. The slaves will get even more coherent in their attacks.

The ship continued to shake and vibrate, but they were still doing more damage to Enigma than Enigma did to them.

And how long until they initiate phase three?

After a couple of taps on her screen, Sparks looked up at him again. *It's been set in motion already. We have fifteen minutes before the psychic blast goes out.*

Seb looked at the vast palace and its multilayers and

shook his head. *Fifteen minutes isn't long enough to blast our way through, is it?*

Sparks shrugged.

So if we want to be certain, the only way we can take their broadcasting device down is to land and go in on foot?

I think that's a safe assumption.

At that moment, a loud *boom* shook the ship. Even in slow motion, Seb only saw the aftermath, so he couldn't blame Reyes for missing it. The explosion of red from the thick cannon blast turned to mist in front of them as all the dials in the ship spun. Alarms sounded and lights flashed before Reyes said, "Hold on. We're going down."

CHAPTER 36

The impact of the ship hitting the ground jolted Seb forward, white light punching through his vision as he connected with the back of Sparks' seat, nose first. Fire flared through his sinuses, and he clapped his hands to his face as he fell to the floor.

The ship had hit the ground so hard, even SA fell over. Sparks and Reyes were strapped into their seats. Seb watched SA stand up, his head spinning. When he felt damp on his top lip, he wiped his nose with the back of his hand to see a trail of blood streaked across it. It could have been a lot worse. Then he looked out of the front windscreen … Enigma's army were running towards them en masse.

One of the large cat-like quadrupeds burst ahead of the pack. It leapt towards them, hitting the windscreen with a *thud*. The glass remained intact. Stronger than the steel hull of the ship, the beast must have seen the futility of attacking from that way because it ran over the top of the vessel, its feet thudding against the roof. A second later a loud *bang* connected with the back door.

More creatures came at them, laying down laser fire as

they charged. The windscreen held, black marks from the blasts but nothing more. They ran past the ship, joining the cat around the back. The vessel shook from their assault.

Only just getting to his feet, his head spinning while his nose leaked blood, Seb held on to Sparks' seat so he didn't fall as it rocked. Vision blurred through watering eyes, he looked around them as if he could find inspiration from the inside of their shuttle.

More footsteps thundered over the top of them. More of the cat-like creatures. They had wide shark's mouths filled with sharp teeth. They had thick jaws loaded with muscles that looked like they could crush rocks. Although, as yet, they hadn't managed to bite through the steel hull of the ship.

The hammering continued against the back door as the front cleared. Sparks stared at her screen before showing it to Seb. The dots of Enigma's army mostly remained in the palace. "They must be protecting the transmitter," she said.

Seb continued to hold on against the shake of their wrecked ship and looked at the scorch marks on their front windscreen. "How long before phase three?"

"Fourteen minutes."

A look at the back door showed Seb it had buckled from the attack driven against it. It wouldn't be long before they busted in. He glanced at SA and Reyes. Both of them stood ready to fight, for what good it would do; they had no chance against the army outside.

An orange glow then dragged Seb's attention away from the back door. Sparks had a blowtorch in her hand. "Where did you get that from?"

She pointed at an open panel. "Most vessels have them. Any active ship needs emergency repairs at some point."

"And what do you plan to do with it?"

Instead of replying, she turned to the wall closest to her

and started to drag a smouldering line down the metal. "Just keep them busy at that end. Hopefully I can open an escape route for us before they realise."

Seb rushed forward and banged against the other side of the door. It seemed to work, the creatures roaring and shouting in response, their blows landing harder than before. The entire ship rocked as if they might turn them over. He banged again and shouted, "Enigma will fall."

A roar unlike any he'd heard before. A deep resonance to it, it made the ship hum from the vibration. Then silence.

Although Seb turned to the others and opened his mouth to speak, something clattered into the ship's door before he could. It hit them so hard, they slid across the stalt desert like a hockey puck.

They came to a halt about fifteen metres away. Fifteen metres closer to the palace. Daylight shone in around the door's seal from where the beast had bent it. It wouldn't hold up to many more attacks like that.

A rush of feet came at them. A second later the army they'd left behind crashed into the back again, shoving them closer to the palace for a second time.

Maybe the same creature, maybe a different one, another deep roar ran a vibration through the soles of Seb's boots. Then the gallop of an almighty beast headed their way. It sounded like it had taken a long run-up.

Boom! It hit the ship again, pushing them closer to the palace. It bent the door, so they could now see out of the gaps between it and its frame. At least forty creatures charged at them.

Before Seb could react, SA and Reyes ran at the gap, poked their blasters out, and opened fire.

Although they fired blind, the screams from the other side suggested they were hitting something.

It gave Seb a moment to look at Sparks as she pulled back a flap of steel. She'd made a gap large enough for them to climb out. She looked at him. "Come on, let's get out of here."

"One of you two hold them off," Seb said to SA and Reyes. "The other one needs to come with me now."

Reyes shoved SA after Seb before returning to the gap in the door.

No time to argue about who went, SA accepted it and followed Seb out of the hole. A large rock of stalt nearby, he ran to it and she followed. The army remained occupied by Reyes around the other side of the ship.

Where Seb had expected to see Sparks come out next, she didn't. "What are they doing?"

Then the shooting stopped. Seb and SA looked at one another.

Reyes burst from the hole with Sparks behind her.

Despite the vociferous cries from Enigma's army, Seb still heard the pulsing bleep. The look in both Reyes' and Sparks' wide eyes confirmed what he thought the noise meant.

Sparks overtook Reyes as the beeps grew louder, skidded behind the rock with Seb and SA, and pressed her back to it to use it as a shield between her and the ship. Reyes slid behind it a second later.

All four of them gasped for breath as they listened to the last tone, a beep longer than the others. It ended with an almighty *boom*. A bright explosion of fire, the heat searing as it blew a strong gust at them. Were it not for the rock they'd shielded themselves behind, they would have melted where they crouched. Scorch marks about ten metres long on either side of them stretched in the direction of the palace.

The mist of vaporised bodies rode on the wind, some of it laying cold pinpricks against Seb's sweating skin.

When the ship crashed down again, the impact of it landing shook the ground.

As the smoke cleared, Seb peered around the rock. None of the soldiers had survived. Very few body parts remained, the blast enough to obliterate most of them. He felt bad for fighting the slaves on the other planets, but any being associating with Enigma deserved everything they got. A look from the wreck to the palace and back again, he patted Sparks' back. "Well done. What did you do?"

"All ships have a self-destruct function."

After nodding at her, Seb said, "Now we need to get into that control room. How long until phase three?"

"Twelve minutes."

CHAPTER 37

SA led this time, bursting out from behind the rock and running across the crystal ground straight at the main entrance to the palace. Enigma's guards knew they were there, so there seemed little point in stealth. Seb followed behind with Reyes and Sparks, watching the grace of his love as she drew one knife for each hand and threw them.

Even with his world slowed down, Seb hadn't seen the guards. Yet, by the time SA's blades reached the palace's entrance, two heads poked out to meet them. The knives landed true, both of them hitting the centre of the guard's faces and burying to the hilt.

Both of Enigma's soldiers fell forwards out into the open. Were they not moving at a flat-out sprint, Seb might have said something, but SA didn't need his compliments. She knew what she could do. They just needed to get inside before they were faced with an army.

SA jumped over the two dead guards, armed herself with two more knives, and threw them into the palace.

Seb heard the sound of laser fire and watched several red traces of it shoot from the palace out across the stalt desert beyond. With Reyes and Sparks beside him, they reached the palace's open entrance in time to see the last guard fall, a line of blaster fire ripping into the ceiling above as it toppled backwards with its finger still on the trigger.

Seb raised his arms over his head as crystal shards rained a sharp spray on top of him. When he pulled them down again, he looked at the back of his forearms to see small pieces embedded in his sleeves. Thankfully he hadn't chosen to wear a T-shirt.

The immediate danger over, Seb looked around the huge open space, gasping as he took it in. The sheer magnificence of the place nearly took his words away. "It looks like something from a fairy tale." He sighed. "It's a shame we have to tear it down." A large open entrance, it had a huge sweeping staircase in the centre with pillars running up either side of it. An almost perfectly square room, it had a first-floor landing running all the way around it. Both the first and ground floors had multiple exits.

Reyes said it before Seb could. "Where are we going, Sparks?"

Although Seb looked at Sparks and watched her open her mouth to reply, he lost sight of her before she spoke. The green-eyed brilliance of the woman in white dragged him into his mind. She stared straight at him. Not angry, but powerful and all-knowing. He and his friends had just entered her domain. She'd been waiting for him.

The woman in white then vanished, and Seb's sight returned. When he looked at the faces of his friends, he saw them all staring at him. A lingering connection with SA, he could see she knew. She'd known all along.

"You okay?" Sparks said. Then, after a second, she helped him out by saying, "We need your call." She pointed at one door and then the one next to it as she said, "Door number one, or door number two?"

The words made sense, but Seb couldn't process them as he looked from one of his friends to the other. As much as he didn't want to say it, he winced and said it anyway. "I have to do something."

"*What?*" Reyes said.

"I need to go. I think I know where Enigma's leader is. I need to go and see her."

Sparks this time. "Why don't we take down their transmitter and rescue Bruke first?"

Shaking his head, Seb looked across all three faces again. "You can do that without me. I *need* to do this." To SA more than any of them, he said, "I've been having visions too. I saw the Pillar of Peace, and then I started to see a woman in white. I think this is why I'm here." Back to the others, he added, "I think if I go, it'll improve your chances of getting to the transmitter and Bruke." SA still hadn't said anything about his visions. He spoke exclusively to her. *Take care of them, yeah? I know you can do this. I'll see you on the other side.*

The blank expression on SA's face threw Seb. Even when pissed off with him, she usually responded. *SA, can you hear me?*

Nothing.

"SA?"

She looked at him.

"I just spoke to you in your head. You can't hear it, can you?"

Crow's feet spread away from the edges of her pinching eyes. A second later, she shook her head.

"It must be something to do with the stalt and the transmitter," Sparks said. "Hopefully if we take the transmitter out, we'll be able to communicate through her again."

"Okay," Seb said. "I'm guessing we'll find each other when this is done."

Although Reyes spoke with a calmness in her voice, her furrowed brow contradicted it. "Surely the fact that we can't communicate is a reason to stay together?"

Seb shook his head. "I need to do this, and I need to do it on my own. I have a feeling that we'll all be in less danger if I go alone. She's waiting for me for some reason. She wants something from me. The least I can do is distract her so you can get on with saving the galaxy from her."

It looked like Reyes might argue, so Seb didn't give her the chance. His attention on SA, he walked over to his love. One thing about being able to speak to one another in their heads meant he didn't have to say anything too personal out loud. While holding her hands, he looked into her bioluminescence. He could get lost in it. "One more fight and this is done. I love you, my sweet."

For a few seconds, SA looked from one of his eyes to the other. Although she couldn't speak, she didn't look like she wanted to. She understood better than anyone. She leaned forward and pressed her warm and full lips against his. For that moment, time stopped.

When SA pulled away, her taste still on his mouth, Seb's heart lifted and he smiled. Everything would work out. It had to. Any more words would ruin it, so he simply turned his back on his friends and ran towards a door leading in the opposite direction to where they were heading.

CHAPTER 38

As Reyes watched Seb run in the opposite direction to where they needed to go, she clenched her jaw and balled her fists. Who the hell did he think he was? How dare he leave them now? They were about to go to war, and he thought the best thing to do was run away. But she still didn't call after him or make any effort to drag him back. If their time together had taught her anything, it was that she could trust him. Whether she thought he'd made the correct call or not didn't matter, she had to focus on her part in all of this and let him do what he needed to.

SA and Sparks—guided by Sparks' map—had already set off. One last glance at Seb as he disappeared through the doorway in the opposite direction to them, Reyes then took off after her friends.

The hard crystal floor sent jarring shocks through Reyes as she ran. Such an unforgiving surface, the violent shock of it felt like it almost kicked back against her steps. Stealth went out of the window too, her boots slamming against the solid ground.

To see SA and Sparks vanish around a corner inspired

Reyes to pick up her pace. It was not the kind of place she wanted to get lost in. When she ran through the next door after them, SA and Sparks had stopped just out of sight. Too slow to react, she went over the top of Sparks and crashed down against the hard ground, the abrasive surface ripping fire along her palms as she put her hands out in front of her and skidded over the rough crystal.

But the pain from the fall vanished when Reyes looked at the room. Her jaw fell loose and her breath caught in her throat. "Where the hell are we?"

SA couldn't answer, and Sparks looked more concerned about getting back to her feet after Reyes had sent her sprawling too. The light on her computer screen suggested it had survived the fall.

After Reyes stood up, she spun on the spot, still at a loss for words. A long rectangular room, it stretched at least ten metres long and three metres wide. Like the entrance to the palace, it had a first-floor landing running around it about two and half metres above them. It looked like there should be doors up there, but she only saw plain walls. The ground floor looked the same. Other than the door they'd entered through, there didn't seem to be any way out.

A loud *shoom* snapped Reyes to attention. The door they'd just run through slammed shut so quickly she'd not even seen it happen. Had she not just entered through it, she wouldn't have believed it had been there in the first place. Although she shared a look with SA and Sparks, none of them spoke. It was like they were all waiting for something worse to occur.

The *shoom* this time rang around the room in stereo. Doors opened all around them: four down each wall on both the ground and first floors. Two opened at each end, save for the one they'd entered. Twenty-three open doors out of a possible twenty-four.

Blaster fire entered the room through every door. Then the guards came in. In Seb's absence, and with SA's lack of communication, Reyes had to lead. The butt of her blaster pressed into her shoulder, she ran at the closest group of soldiers.

About ten guards in their close proximity, when shots flew from behind Reyes, it told her SA and Sparks were backing her up. She pulled her trigger, her entire body shaking with the blasts.

Although Reyes focused on their closest attackers, she had an awareness of the room filling with soldiers. Suddenly all the doors slid shut again. They now had no way out.

While they focused on the ten or so guards closest to them, blaster fire came their way from what must have been at least one hundred soldiers now in the locked room. Shards of stalt exploded from the walls, nearly as deadly as the laser fire that had birthed them. They stood no chance. So much for a plan of action; when Reyes looked around, she said, "We're screwed."

SA couldn't respond, and Sparks didn't. Instead, the small Thrystian slipped a pair of dark goggles over her eyes, fished something from her pocket, and threw it into the middle of the room.

The grenade tinkled against the stalt floor as it rolled for a second before coming to a halt. The chaos of gunfire stopped.

Whoom! The grenade released a magnesium brilliance, the crystal around it magnifying the already dazzling glare. It glowed so brightly, it damn near set fire to Reyes' eyes, rendering her useless as she clapped her hands to her face and fell to the ground. Out of breath, blind, and with her heart galloping, she then felt the touch of a long hand against her shoulder. "Stay here. Everything will be fine," Sparks said. "Your sight will return."

Reyes had no choice but to trust her friend. As she lay on the ground, her pulse fast, her throat dry, she focused on her breaths. The only way to ground herself, she fought against her frantic thoughts. Nothing but white in her vision, she listened to what must have been Sparks fire her blaster. The only blaster to go off in the room, she must have been the only being in the entire place who could see.

While the shooting continued, Reyes rubbed her eyes and blinked. Utterly ineffective, she had to do something other than lie there. A hard bite on her bottom lip—so hard it stung—stopped her from calling out to Sparks. Too much noise and she'd be a target for the guards, something for the blind to aim their weapons at.

As the sound of blaster fire continued unrelenting, Reyes put her energy into muttering near silent support for her friend. "You can do it, Sparks. I trust in you."

CHAPTER 39

As much as Seb hadn't wanted to leave the others, they'd be fine. They knew what they needed to do, and they'd find a way to do it. They could stop the broadcast, but he had to stop Enigma. He didn't know much about what lay ahead, but he knew that.

Seb ran on intuition, not knowing where to go until a moment before he had to decide. Every long hallway looked the same. Every turn like the one he'd taken before. Yet he ploughed forward through the palace, turning left, right, right, left, left, right without breaking stride.

Finally Seb's scenery changed as he ran into one of the palace's many spires. A circular turret, he looked up at the pointed roof at least ten storeys above him. Stairs corkscrewed around the walls, showing him the route to the top. For a second, his legs refused to carry him any farther. Something about climbing so high on transparent stairs … But he dug deep, shoved down his reluctance, and pushed on. The woman in his vision had to be up there.

Near dizzy from his fast and twisting ascent, Seb tried to focus on the next few steps ahead and not much farther. No rail to stop him, if he slipped and fell, his body would shatter on the hard ground below. He got so fixed on where to put his feet, he didn't see the guards until it was too late.

Two of them—centaur-like creatures with four legs and two arms and shields as tall as they were—blocked his path. Then they charged, coming down the stairs to meet him as he came up. Just a few metres between them, they closed the gap quickly and drove their shields into him, sending him back several wobbly steps before he lost his footing and fell.

The second the back of Seb's head connected with one of the stairs, a loud ring sang through his skull and his world turned dark.

CHAPTER 40

Reyes' ears rang from the constant sound of shattering stalt. Enigma's army must have been blind like her. They must have realised if they didn't shoot back, they'd be executed by Sparks' blasts.

Splash after splash, the shots hit the room at random points in quick succession. It made Reyes' head spin and her heart gallop. One of them had to hit her soon, but what could she do? Nothing but whiteness in her vision, she had no choice but to rely on Sparks.

The only chance she had of protecting herself, Reyes lay face down, her nose squashed against the cold stalt floor while she covered the back of her head with her hands. Not only did she experience the vibration of every explosion through her face, but she felt the stinging spray of shattered stalt against her back.

Despite the disorientating wash of sound, the next explosion Reyes heard rang louder than all the others. A heavy *whoosh* filled the room, the reverberation of the noise swelling through the grand hall. A moment later, a loud *bang!*

Whatever hit the floor, it landed so hard the vibration of it shook her face and made her eyes water.

"Sparks!" Reyes shouted, lifting her head to look in the direction she expected her friend to be in. Before she could say anything else, another *whoosh* and *bang* drowned her out.

Maybe Reyes imagined it, but when she looked up again, it seemed like some of the whiteness in her eyes had turned slightly grey. Where she'd seen nothing, she could now see movement. Although still no more than shifting shadows. "Sparks?" Still nothing.

Reyes got to her feet on shaking legs, her arms stretched out in front of her. Blaster fire and the glassy crash of stalt exploded around the room. Less than before, but splinters of the sharp crystal still hit her, making her flinch when they landed against her face.

"Sparks?" Reyes stumbled forward, caught her foot on what felt like a large rock of stalt, and fell to the ground again. Expecting to impact it sooner than she did, she put her hands out and braced for the shock. When it came a second later, it caught her body off guard and sent a jarring jolt snapping through her.

After hitting the floor, Reyes rolled over as if she could squirm free from the nauseating burn the fall had forced beneath her shoulder blades. How could she possibly help Sparks if she could be defeated by a lump of rock?

Then the shooting stopped. An eerie stillness swelled through the room. Reyes lay blind on the cold floor, trying to see the shadows in the grey. Nothing moved. At least nothing she could see. "Sparks?" Her voice echoed, the desperation in her tone coming back at her from the hard walls.

Then the sound of footsteps. They came towards her fast. Reyes saw something. A shape, nothing more. She flinched.

Just before Reyes' attacker clattered into her, she felt a hand on the top of her head. She gasped.

"It's okay," Sparks said. "It's okay."

Sideswiped by her emotion, a lump swelled in Reyes' throat, hot tears streaming down her cheeks a second later. She sniffed against her running nose and looked up in the direction of the voice. "What the hell happened?" The panic she'd pushed down rushed forward, and she shouted before she'd had a chance to control it. "I can't see. I'm blind."

"Shhhhhhh," Sparks said and stroked her head. "It's temporary. I can help you get your sight back. Sorry I couldn't do it before. Different species react differently, and I needed to capitalise on the advantage I had by taking the guards down before they recovered. This won't smell nice, but it'll work."

"What won't smell nice?"

It sounded like a small bottle being unscrewed. Reyes then caught the medicinal alcohol smell of whatever Sparks put in front of her. The second she inhaled, the scent ran up her nostrils and drove a hard kick through her heart.

CHAPTER 41

Seb's heart kicked, forcing both his eyes wide and the air from his lungs. A centaur creature—a muscular semi-naked brute of a thing—glared at him through neon pink orbs as it stepped away. Hooves clicking against the hard stalt ground, it looked like one of the guards that had shoved him down the stairs. As it backed off, it closed its grip around the small bottle it had held to Seb's nose.

The galloping high initiated by the beast's ointment quickened Seb's pulse and sent needles into his brain. But as his consciousness returned, he suddenly saw her, and everything slowed to an almost halt. The green-eyed woman.

Still not entirely sure where they were, the battering wind told Seb they were high up. Immobile, he watched the woman in white shoo the two centaurs away. She clearly didn't feel threatened by Seb, and she clearly wanted to be alone with him.

The wind cut to Seb's core. Fierce and bitter from where it had gathered speed racing over Varna's stalt desert. A natural instinct to hug himself for warmth, his arms didn't move when he tried to pull them in. A look to either side showed him he'd been strapped to what appeared to be a cross of some sort. His arms were bound at the wrists to the horizontal pole, his ankles clamped together and tied to the upright one. The ropes were pulled tight enough for both his hands and feet to tingle from where the circulation had been cut off. Although he wanted to speak to the woman, he resisted the urge, his heart rate settling as he stared straight at her.

The green-eyed lady waited for a few seconds, but her patience ran out first. A wry smile, her long white hair billowed in the breeze as she said, "Don't you want to know who I am?"

A sneer, it took all Seb had to not spit at her. Besides, the fierce wind would probably throw it back in his face if he did. "What does it matter? You're a *murderer*."

"You think it's that simple?" She threw her head back and laughed at the sky. Where her eyes had glowed before, they were on fire when she looked at him again. "You've been a victim of the news cycle for far too long, Sebastian Zodo. Killer, saint. Soldier, terrorist. Black, white. That's all they give you credit for understanding. They want to give you a simplified identity and then set you against the other side so you don't notice all the shit they're pulling right under your nose. They busy you with extremes while they play the beat you subconsciously march to. And maybe they're right to do so. Maybe it's all most beings can understand. But I think you're better than that." She lowered her voice. "So I'm here to tell you the galaxy has far more nuance than those in power want you to believe."

Seb tested his bonds by tugging against them. If anything, they tightened. "Spare me your crap and just kill me if that's what you're going to do."

"I want you to come on a journey with me, Sebastian."

"Stop calling me that."

"The kind of name that's only reserved for family, right?"

Seb scoffed a laugh at her. "What? You're telling me you're family now?" For the first time since he'd woken, he glanced out over the roof of the palace and saw the spire he'd looked at when they flew in, the thick one with the large open space beside it. Even before he got there, he'd recognised it as where he'd end up.

Instead of replying to him, the woman's green eyes lost focus, and she frowned as she concentrated. A second later, Seb lost sight of her as the world changed in front of him although he still heard her voice.

"Recognise this?"

It took the breath from Seb's lungs to watch two little boys playing on a sandy wooden floor. All of the floors in Danu were sandy. He watched as he played with Davey. He must have been about three at the time. They had toy soldiers lined up in front of each other. They were playing battles. They liked to play battles. As the youngest, he always lost because Davey made the rules. Tears itched his eyes to look at his now dead brother. His voice cracked when he shouted at the woman in white, "How are you doing this?"

Instead of replying to him, she changed what he saw. Where he'd been looking at the two boys, it moved to show him his dad, red-faced while pointing a finger at a woman. The woman was about the same age as his dad. They were both in their forties. She had long white hair, flowing white clothes, and brilliant green eyes. "What are *you* doing there?"

"I used to call you Sebastian as a boy. Sebastian and David. Do you know that? Your dad hated it. Your father and I always had a difficult relationship."

The argument between Seb's dad and the woman with the

green eyes increased in ferocity, spittle flying from his dad's mouth as his face grew redder and he leaned close to her.

"What are you doing in my family home?" Seb said.

"I used to be welcome there. Until that day. I think it was the paranoia of the prophecy that got to your dad. Not something I had to live with. That was all his. Well, all yours now."

The green-eyed woman then left the room, and the vision followed her. It played like a movie, the camera fixing on whatever the director thought Seb should see. "You expect me to believe you're related to him? What do you think—?" But he lost his speech as he watched his mother walk from another room to meet the woman with the green eyes. The word left him in a gasp. "Mum?"

What had been silent footage suddenly had sound, and Seb heard his mother's voice as she spoke to the green-eyed woman. "Take care of yourself. I'm sure he'll come around." It didn't matter what she said, more that it tore into his heart to hear her voice again. "He just needs some time," his mum went on to say. Were it not for the cross he'd been strapped to, Seb would have fallen hard from the strength having left his body.

Seb watched as his mum and the green-eyed woman hugged. Then he watched the green-eyed woman walk from the house out of the front door.

The sound of the wind came back to him, crashing against the side of his face, sending a poorly timed drum roll battering through his ears. The woman with the green eyes stood in front of him in her current form. In her sixties now, she looked as pure as she had in her forties. "Your mum understood where I was coming from. And she promised me she'd let me keep in touch with you two. After all, I wanted to be in the lives of my nephews as they grew up."

Unable to reply, Seb's head dropped. He looked at the glistening crystal ground, his warm tears turning cold against his face in the harsh wind.

CHAPTER 42

For a brief moment Reyes worried it might never happen, but as her sight gradually recovered, she slowed her breaths to bring her panic down. A tight pain in her chest, her body tense, she looked at Sparks standing over her. Tiny cuts covered the small Thrystian's face like freckles. The spray from the crystal must have eaten into her as she fought Enigma's guards. But the wounds looked to be superficial. Sore, but superficial. The same couldn't be said for Enigma's army. A glance around the room showed her that the place looked like the streets of Kajan, bodies and body parts scattered everywhere. When she nodded at her, Sparks nodded back and turned her attention to SA. Clearly going through the same adjustment, the yellow-skinned assassin rubbed her eyes as if it would bring her sight back quicker.

Because Sparks focused on SA, Reyes looked around the room again. The shock of it made her laugh, and she shook her head. When she spoke, her voice echoed in the near silent space. "You certainly did a number on this room."

Sparks shrugged before she scratched her head while

raising her eyebrows. "I needed to take drastic action. There were a *lot* of them."

Other than the clear massacre of the army, Sparks had also demolished the place. The landing running around the first floor remained intact above them and nowhere else. The rest of it had been shattered and gathered on the floor in large piles of glistening rocks. It must have been what had caused the whooshing sounds.

"Sorry I blinded you both," Sparks said, pulling Reyes' attention back to her. "I had a hunch the flash bang would be effective in here and knew it would be the best chance of taking Enigma's army down. But I couldn't warn you about it. Especially as we can't talk through SA at the moment. If I'd have told you to cover your eyes, they might have done the same."

After watching SA nod, Reyes spoke for both of them. "It's fine. You did what you had to. And it worked better than any other plan we had."

"It was the best we had, right?" Sparks said.

Reyes smiled. "Right."

Her computer still working, Sparks held it up for Reyes and SA to see. "The main control room isn't far. We have six minutes to get in there and destroy their transmitter. I'd like to give you more time to recover, but we need to go."

While Reyes nodded, SA got to her feet. Later than her to regain her sight, yet she seemed more ready to move off. Another laugh thrown back at her in the quiet room, she shook her head. "You're a machine, SA."

The usual warmth had left SA's eyes. Steel belied her calm bioluminescence. Whatever it took, she'd make sure the next phase of Enigma's plan didn't get implemented. The next broadcast wouldn't happen.

No time to waste, Reyes took Sparks' hand when she

offered it to her to help her up. She then tried to find strength in her weak legs as she set off after her two friends.

Powdered stalt crunched beneath Reyes' every step, and she watched the floor to avoid the larger divots dug into it from the firefight. It slowed their progress, but better that than falling and breaking an ankle.

Every door now open again like when the guards had entered, Reyes watched Sparks and SA run out of one of the exits in the left wall. She followed them out a second later to find them both stopped in front of her and halted just short of clattering into them for a second time. When she looked where they were looking, she gasped. "Damn!"

Bruke sat on the other side of a thick window of stalt. It gave them a clear view of him strapped to a large chair with an Enigma guard standing in front of him. It held a saw in its hand. The blade of it had a coating of rust and blood.

When Bruke saw them, his eyes widened. Although his mouth stretched open, the thick window muted his scream. Whatever the guard had said to him, it must have been making good on its promise. It leaned over him with the saw and cut into his left thigh.

Before any of them could speak, Sparks opened fire on the window, screaming as she laid down a barrage of blasts against it. The transparent barrier took all her shots, a series of black marks to show for it, but nothing else.

After she'd swapped her gun for her computer, Sparks projected a red lined grid against the window. "Damn it. Whatever they've used to make this, it'll take a cannon to destroy it."

Although Sparks lifted her screen for them to see, Reyes couldn't take her eyes from Bruke. A twist writhed through her insides to watch more blood coat the guard's rusty saw. It put all its weight into each hacking cut. Veins stood out on Bruke's neck from the effort of his scream.

"*Reyes!*"

It snapped her away from Bruke and onto Sparks.

"*Focus!* I'm going to get Bruke out of there. I can see the route to get to him. You and SA need to take down the transmitter without me. Okay?"

Another look at Bruke, Reyes watched his eyes roll and then his head fall limp as he passed out.

"Okay?" Sparks said again.

Her head spinning from what she'd seen, Reyes looked at SA, but she couldn't focus. A million and one traumas from her time as a marine flooded back. The *Faradis* sat front and centre of those memories. She'd seen too much suffering on the faces of those she cared about. It took for her to shake her head to get the thoughts away. It wouldn't help them now. "I'm sorry, my head's a mess." She turned to SA. "Can you remember the way?"

SA nodded, the same steely look in her eyes.

"Okay," Reyes said.

Sparks took control again. "I'll see you both outside when this is over. Good luck."

CHAPTER 43

Not only did Seb have to deal with the burn of the tightly bound ropes on his wrists and ankles, but the base of his neck ached from where he hung his head. Yet he didn't lift it, keeping it slumped as if it were too heavy to hold. While staring at the floor, the harsh wind continued to crash into him, bullying his limp frame. His throat ached, his nose ran, and his view of the world blurred through his tears.

The woman in front of Seb stepped forward, her long white robes covering what would be his view of her feet. A gentle touch with a warm hand, she placed two fingers beneath his chin and lifted it so he faced her. His aunty smiled at him, and for the first time, he saw the familial resemblance. He saw her love for him. Compassion in her green eyes, she spoke in a gentle voice. "Are you wondering why your dad pushed me away?"

Seb tried to speak, but it came out as a croak. He nodded instead.

While stroking his face, the soothing touch of her soft fingers making Seb push into it like a cat enjoying the affection, she said, "It's because of now. *This* moment."

The same sensation as before, the green-eyed woman showed Seb another memory.

Seb's head spun to watch the woman in front of him and his mum. They were inside, but he couldn't see where. Not that it mattered. "Just give him time," his mum said to her.

The vision came to an abrupt end, forcing a gasp from Seb. Back on the roof of the palace, he blinked against his tears and the biting breeze. Although he opened his mouth, his aunt cut him off.

"Your mum was behind me with this," she said. "She knew what needed to be done, and she tried to help your dad see it. But he refused. He couldn't see clearly because of our upbringing. He said Mum and Dad always loved me more. And maybe they did, but that had nothing to do with what I was trying to say to him. What your mum was trying to say to him."

Still nothing to give, Seb simply stared at her. His hot grief leaked from his eyes.

"Your mum was amazing. She saw where I was coming from. She knew how we could stop the darkness spreading through the galaxy."

The words crashed into Seb. *The darkness in the galaxy.* It had to be stopped, and he'd been the one prophesied to do it. It had to be the reason he'd found her. Then he thought about their battle on Aloo. Then all of the footage Sparks had shown him of the carnage in the galaxy. Of the massacre on Kajan. The dead bodies everywhere. "But you've killed *thousands*, if not more. You're still killing them with the chaos you've let loose. You promote slavery."

"We're toppling regimes, Seb; we're not killing."

"You *are* killing."

"Death is an unfortunate by-product of what we're doing. We're trying to change a tyrannical regime that sees most of the power in the galaxy held by just a few. It's a dictatorship wearing democracy's clothes. We have to bring down societies before we can show them a new way. It's the only chance we have of making a change. Those in power have too much of a stranglehold." She made a motion with her hands as if snapping an invisible twig. "We have to break that."

Seb continued to cry as he looked at her.

"The darkness in the galaxy is inequality," she said. "The light is justice. I can't do this on my own. Your mum would be with me here now if she'd made it this far. I need you beside me, Seb, so we can take down the monopolies that control everything. You think you know what slavery is? Take a look at how they use the promise of credits in exchange for labour to keep people just above the poverty line. They make beings work their fingers and hooves to the bone just so they can eat for another week. Just so they don't let their families starve. There's enough resources to go around, so there's no need for them to behave like that."

"But you worked with the Countess."

"I needed an army, and she could give it to me. I would have killed her if you hadn't."

A look from his bonds then back to the woman, Seb let her continue.

"I can see it in your eyes. You know why your mum was on my side. I hate that we have to break so many things to rebuild a better world, but change doesn't come without a revolution kick-starting it."

Seb watched his aunty pull a knife from her belt as she walked towards him. She slipped the blade beneath the ropes around his ankles and then the ones around his wrists. A sharp pull each time and the ropes fell away, relieving the pressure with a tingling rush of blood back into his feet and hands.

After Seb had toppled from the cross, his knees stinging from where they took the weight of his fall, his aunty helped him stand and wrapped him in a tight hug. She smelled of lavender. "I'm giving you this because your mum can't. You still have family that love you, Seb."

Broken by his sobbing, Seb lifted his arms and hugged her back.

CHAPTER 44

"I thought it would be harder to get here," Reyes said, slightly out of breath from the run.

SA looked at her, unable to respond.

A window on their left gave them a view into the ballroom with the transmitter in the centre of it. It stood as a large metal antenna at least four metres tall. Take that down and they could get out of there. Reyes looked at the empty room it sat in. "And we've done it with time to spare." She rested against a nearby wall. "Just let me get my breath back."

They had to walk down a short corridor to access the ballroom. Two more doors between them and stopping Enigma. All of the others had opened automatically. Everything had been a little too easy. However, despite having to keep their guard raised, they didn't yet have a good reason to stop. They couldn't defend against a bad feeling. Until it became more tangible, they had to keep going.

One final deep inhale to fill her lungs, Reyes nodded at SA and walked towards the penultimate door. It opened with a *whoosh,* but before she could step through it, SA grabbed her left bicep in a hard grip and dragged her back. It forced

Reyes to pull in a sharp breath, her anger spiking in reaction to the pain. It settled when she looked at her friend. First, SA wouldn't hurt her unless she had a very good reason. Second, SA would kick her arse if it came to trading blows. Still irritable, she shrugged as she twisted from SA's grip and said, "What?"

When SA pointed through the window, Reyes saw it. "Oh."

Two doors at the other end of the large room where they hadn't been a moment ago. Much like the long room Sparks had obliterated, the doors were invisible until they weren't. A seemingly unending line of guards ran in through each one. They moved into the room and spread out, filling one end and holding their weapons at the ready. Although, it didn't look like they'd seen Reyes and SA yet.

While watching them, Reyes let go of a long exhale. "It looks like we have a battle on our hands, then."

A sharp shake of her head, SA pointed her own thumb at her chest.

It took all Reyes had to stop herself from laughing. "You think I'm going to let you in there on your *own*?"

A nod this time. It suggested Reyes didn't have a choice.

"Why would I do that?"

At that moment, SA raised her right hand. She held the leveller in it. When Reyes saw she had the pin in her left, it took a second for her to find her words. Unable to take her eyes from the armed explosive, she finally said, "Oh my. When did you decide this was a suicide mission?"

Obviously SA didn't reply.

"Surely there are other options."

SA's fine and crescent-shaped eyebrows lifted as she looked from Reyes to the guards rushing into the ballroom.

The glint of crystal everywhere, Reyes had never seen a building so beautiful, and they were going to destroy it.

At least one hundred guards in the room now, more were still coming in. The two of them stood no chance if they wanted to fight them. But she couldn't let SA die alone.

Just before Reyes could speak, SA did. "I need to do this on my own."

It sent Reyes stumbling back a couple of steps. She'd never heard her talk before. Other than singing, she didn't think any of the others had heard her voice either. "You ... you can talk?"

SA stepped towards Reyes and stared into her eyes. With a pinch of her brow, she spoke. Her voice sounded like it belonged to an angel. "Please, let me do this. You can see we won't survive. It makes more sense for one of us to die than it does for both of us. And either way, I'm going in there."

"What about Seb?"

Tears filled her brilliant eyes before she looked at the ground. Drops fell from her face to the stalt below. "Believe me, I've thought about that. I love him more than any other being I've ever met, but I can't be so selfish as to put my happiness before the fate of the galaxy."

"You don't have to."

"Huh?"

"Let me do it."

It took several shakes of SA's head before she finally said, "No. This was my idea. I'd rather die myself than live with the guilt of sending you in there."

Her head still spinning, Reyes tried to find an appropriate response. She looked from the grenade in SA's hand back to her friend's grief-buckled face. When SA took a slow step towards the room with the guards in it, the door to the small corridor opened again.

Reyes followed. "I can't let you do this on your own."

"Don't be a fool, Reyes." SA took another step away.

"We can find a way out. We can destroy the transmitter and survive this. Look at all of the other things we've made it through. Why not this?"

A slight sag to her frame, SA shook her head. "Look at it in there."

Reyes looked to her left through the window again and watched more guards flood into the place. They hadn't seen her or SA yet. When they did, it would be game over. But they were the Shadow Order. They always found a way. Besides, she'd lost too many people; she couldn't lose any more.

Had Reyes not been watching the guards, she would have seen it before it happened. Instead, it took for the whoosh of the automatic door closing for Reyes to look back at SA on the other side of it.

Reyes lunged for the sensor to open the door again, but before she could trigger it, SA shot the control panel on the other side, locking the door in place.

Steel in her eyes, SA stared through the small window at Reyes, her beautiful voice muffled because of the barrier between them. "You don't have a choice now."

While looking from SA to the guards, Reyes started to cry. "What are you doing?"

"I'm doing this on my own. Tell Seb I love him." SA looked to her right. Enigma's army came forward in a wave. Her voice quickened when she said, "Now go. Save yourself and get our friends off this cursed planet. They need you much more than I do right now. You'll be more useful to them than you will dying in here."

Despite remaining in front of the door in the hope it would somehow open, Reyes quickly gave up. A blurred view of her friend, she watched the yellow-skinned woman raise her grenade at the window to the ballroom. The guards needed to see what she'd come armed with. They slowed their charge towards her.

SA then pressed her palm against the small window separating them. Reyes pressed the other side, the touch of the glass cold.

"I'll give you two minutes to get out of here," SA said. "Any more than that and I'll be pushing my luck."

When SA pulled her hand away and made a shooing motion with it, Reyes nodded at her friend, blew her a kiss, turned around, and ran away from her. Tears ran down her face, and her weak legs barely carried her, but she had to get out of there. The others might need her. SA was right: there seemed little point in all of them dying.

CHAPTER 45

While Seb stood on the roof, holding his aunt, a deep sadness crashed into him. It forced him back a few steps. The contact of anyone would have been too much, especially her, a stranger. His hand covering his heart, he tried to ride out its now erratic beat. A feeling he'd never felt before. His head spun as he tried to make sense of it. Pain and suffering, it almost overwhelmed him. A drop more and he wouldn't be able to hold it in his heart. His mind then separated from his body, leaving his physical form behind with her on the cold and blustery roof.

Like a bird taking flight, Seb's consciousness flew over the top of the vast and beautiful stalt palace. When it got to the edge of the structure, it dived, dropping down before it doubled back and entered via the foyer he'd been in earlier. Instead of going the way he'd gone before, he flew in the direction his friends had gone.

Through the first doorway, Seb came to a long rectangular room. Even with the devastation—the dead bodies and the shattered stalt—he could see how it had once been a place of beauty.

Something guided Seb and he let it. It dragged him through one of the many open doorways. Then he suddenly stopped. A noise halfway between a gasp and a moan left him as if his consciousness had been on the receiving end of a gut punch. When he got his words back, he said, "Mum?"

A smile more radiant than he'd ever seen from her before, she stepped towards him and held her graceful hands in his direction. He grabbed them, his view of her blurring through his tears.

"You're okay, sweetie. You've come to the right place," she said. "You've come home."

The cold wind crashed into Seb again, dragging him back to the roof. He now held his aunty's hands like he'd held his mum's. While staring at her, a vivid green glow looking back at him, he said, "That was you in the palace?"

"Your mum lives on in me, Seb. When she was alive, we were close and we spoke often. I know her as well as any being."

Seb's breaths slowed, and some of the tension left his upper body. The pain of loss he'd always carried in his chest eased a little for the experience he'd had. Then he looked at his aunty again, the world in front of him blurring through his tears. "I don't know what's real anymore."

"This is," his aunty said as she squeezed his grip. Her hands were warm and soft. They gave him something to cling onto on the cold roof. "This moment right now is real. We're on the verge of something great here. We're about to reset the galaxy. We're going to demolish poverty and inequality. You'll be a hero. Your mum would be so proud of you."

For every second Seb held his aunty's hands, the pain that had forced his consciousness from his body abated. Almost like she could control it if he let her; like she could give him a truth she wanted him to see. She could show him his mum whenever she chose to. What would he have seen in the palace if he hadn't met her there? But it made sense for them to end poverty. His head spinning, he barely knew up from down when he said, "What do you need from me?"

"It's not what *I* need; it's what we must do to heal the galaxy."

"But how? What can *I* do? I keep being told I'm the chosen one, but I know nothing. I can't do anything special. Not compared to what our ancestors were capable of."

A shake of her head, her white hair dancing on the breeze, Seb's aunty stepped closer and encompassed him with her warmth. The smile he couldn't see was evident in her voice. "You're so much more than anyone before you. You just don't realise it. You saw me when I was reaching out to you, didn't you?"

Seb flashed back to when the first transmission went out and he'd seen the Pillar of Peace like SA had. Then when he'd touched it on Kajan. "Yeah, I did."

"Not only do you have psychic powers, Seb, but they're so strong in you; you're a transmitter too."

"A what?"

"I can help the revolutionaries take over the planets they're on. If we work together, we can make this a peaceful transition."

"But I've seen the chaos out there. The chaos *you've* unleashed."

"Until now, I've had to use the transmitter in the palace. It's clumsy and basic. With you beside me, I can reach so many more revolutionaries. I can help them make the right choices. I can guide them in real time. The only reason they're running riot is because stalt is a poor alternative to using you for getting the message out. Together we can guide the revolution. We can restore peace, and when we do, it will be a fairer, more just galaxy for *everyone*."

"Nothing's making sense to me anymore."

His hands still in hers, Seb's aunty squeezed them again, her voice running through his mind as a soft whisper. Her words loosened his muscles like he'd stepped into a warm bath. "Just let go. Trust me like you would your own mother."

A tingling ran through his hands. The same tingling he felt when he healed someone; the same magic at work. She could help him unlock what he had inside. She could help him fulfil his destiny.

CHAPTER 46

Barely the energy to put one foot in front of the other, Reyes almost fell into every step as she ran. The hard stalt floor sent shocks up her legs. Her knees—already sore with fatigue—burned with a deep, throbbing ache.

Every corridor in the place looked the same. Reyes thought she was heading back the way she came from, but she couldn't be sure. It didn't help that she had to view everything through tear-blurred eyes. But she had to keep moving forward. SA would hold onto the leveller for as long as she could. Still, it wouldn't be long enough. They had about ninety seconds at best.

Just before Reyes ran around the next corner, she heard the laboured breaths of another being. She stopped. The heavy slaps of her feet would be a dead giveaway of her approach if she hadn't already blown her cover. The butt of her blaster wedged into her shoulder, she fought against her exhaustion, blinked away her blurred vision, drew a deep gasp, and stepped towards the bend and the being on the other side of it.

Not in the best frame of mind for a one-woman gunfight,

Reyes didn't have the luxury of time to prepare herself. The second-best option had to be surprise. She jumped around the corner and aimed her blaster at the creature. Before she pulled the trigger, she stopped. "Sparks?" When she looked at the small Thrystian's sweaty face, her heart sank. She looked defeated. Hardly surprising considering what she'd had to carry. "Bruke?" she said and squatted down next to him, her legs on fire with fatigue. "What have they done to you?"

His left leg completely gone, Bruke's eyes rolled from him fighting to remain conscious. He looked at his wound before turning his attention to Reyes. "Sparks …" He drifted off.

"I had to cauterise it to stop it bleeding out," Sparks said. "I'm not sure I got to him in time."

Reyes ruffled her nose at the smell of burned flesh and said, "He's still alive, so you got to him in time." Because Sparks had used both of her hands to move Bruke, he held onto her computer for her. The timer on the screen read one minute and fifty-two seconds, fifty-one, fifty …

Reyes shook her head while watching it and said, "We've got less time than that. SA's going to blow the transmitter and the palace up with it."

The look in Sparks' eyes suggested she'd already given up, so Reyes pulled Bruke's left arm around her shoulders. Grimacing from the strain of supporting him, she said, "Lead the way to their hangar. We need a ship to get out of here. We'll make it."

"What about SA?"

The question made Bruke's weight seem to double across her shoulders. Reyes shook her head and gasped from her effort and emotional exhaustion. "She's not coming."

Sparks stared at her.

"If she's going to blow the transmitter and the palace up, she has to be there."

"Has to?"

"There were hundreds of soldiers there. We couldn't fight them, so she decided to arm the leveller. She locked me out so I couldn't follow her. She's going to hold the army back for as long as she can. When she goes down, the grenade will go off."

The spread of Sparks' purple eyes was magnified by her glasses.

"Come on, Sparks," Reyes said. "SA sacrificed herself for us, the least we can do is have the decency to survive."

The small Thrystian nodded, pulled her computer from Bruke's hands, and tapped against the screen. A map appeared. "It's not far," she said as she set off ahead of them, her blaster drawn.

A dead weight on her, Reyes might have hated every second of her marine training, but it now came in handy as much as it ever had. You had to be able to carry your brother as far as was necessary to save their life. The crystal floors helped. It meant she could drag Bruke.

Three short corridors later and none of Enigma's army in sight, they arrived at the hangar. The space looked to take up half of the palace's footprint. A vast stalt floor, tall walls, and a high ceiling, the hangar had a fleet of ships of all shapes and sizes.

Still taking the lead, Sparks ran over to a small vessel. Large enough to get them and Seb out of there if they found him, but small enough to be effective in a dogfight. She used her computer to open the back while she ran at it.

While gasping, Reyes laid Bruke down in the back of the ship before leaning over him and kissing his head. "Hold on in there."

"You flying?" Sparks said.

Before Reyes could reply, she looked across the hangar and caught sight of a line of mechs. She shook her head. "No. I'm going to fly one of them. Two ships in this fight are better than one. Let's find Seb and get the hell out of here."

A moment's pause, Reyes then leaned close to Sparks and kissed the top of her head too.

Already wide purple eyes widened as Sparks looked up at her.

While Reyes stepped towards the ship's exit, a loud explosion went off in the direction of the ballroom. It shook the ground. The hope she'd held onto that SA would be okay vanished with the earth-trembling detonation. Popping and cracking stalt—she shook her head as the sounds of the failing structure caught up to the large hangar. She called behind her as she ran at the mechs, "We've got to get out of here now!"

CHAPTER 47

The tingling that had started in Seb's hands ran up his arms. Vines of energy, they seeped into him, intoxicating in their languid and warm-honeyed crawl through his being. A slightly woozy feeling as the wind rocked him. The tingling sensation then reached the sadness in his heart. The sadness he'd felt a moment ago when driven back from his aunty. The pain of every being in the galaxy. Of their loss. He let go of his aunt's hands and stepped back again.

Serene as she looked at him, his aunty frowned, her long flowing gown riding the elements. "What's wrong, dear?"

Without realising it, Seb had put his hand to his heart. It did nothing to dilute the darkness swelling through it. "How do you know this is the right way to do things? Why destroy societies? I mean, should you be going to all these planets and overthrowing governments when you can change things peacefully?"

"That's what we're doing. You're helping me so we can take the violence out of the revolutionaries. You're helping me talk to more of the slaves, to guide them to do the right thing."

Something in her voice didn't ring true. Her words were accelerated with the slightly frantic sound of desperation. "But we're still taking their planets by force. It doesn't seem right. There *has* to be a democratic solution."

"What? You think we should go to those in power and ask them politely to give it up?" Scorn in her tone, she shook her head. "You think those benefiting most from the way things are will stand aside while we disempower them? Your mum knew better. She saw what we had to do."

It made sense, those in power wouldn't give it up.

"Democracy doesn't exist in this galaxy. Our lives are controlled by the games the rich and powerful play. They sell us the illusion of choice, but it's not real."

"But what's the alternative? We replace their leadership with *your* leadership?"

"*Our* leadership."

It was like she was trying to sell him on being in power. He craved a quiet life with—

An explosion then sounded out. The palace shook beneath Seb's feet. He saw for the first time something he hadn't before. A flicker in her green calm. The look of deceit. Something about the explosion had pierced the veil. He stepped back another pace.

The sound of cracking stalt possessed the palace. Loud pops raced through the structure as it failed.

As much as his aunt looked like she wanted to project calm, she'd clearly been rattled. A bitterness had risen up from inside her. She thrust her hands in his direction, her charm gone. "We need to do this *now*. Come on, help me contact the revolutionaries before those in power take it back. Help me do what your mother wanted to help me with all those years ago."

Seb stepped back again. The sadness he'd felt only a

minute or two ago resurfaced. Stronger than before and somehow more personal. It swelled through him. Something had gone seriously wrong. Something irreversible and his aunt knew exactly what.

CHAPTER 48

The cracking and popping of the palace's failing structure chased Reyes through the vast hangar. The entire place could come crashing down at any moment and end them all. Where she'd felt fatigued before, adrenaline now spurred her on, surging through her as she ran. The line of mechs in her sight helped her move. Get to one of them and she'd be home free.

Another sound came to Reyes over the noise of the palace falling apart; the stampede of boots.

One eye on the way they'd come from, Reyes saw the first of Enigma's army appear. Halfway between Sparks' ship and the mechs, she stopped. Those in the ballroom might be dead, but the palace clearly had more guards.

As she watched more of Enigma's army stream into the hangar, Reyes looked at Sparks' ship again. It would be easier to run back to it. She could get out of there with them. But before she moved, the army opened fire on it and the back of Sparks' ship closed. The small vessel's shields repelled the attack, the blaster fire ineffective against it. For now. Sparks would have to get out of there before a soldier with a larger gun arrived.

The *whoosh* of Sparks' ship's boosters rumbled through the hangar as she lifted the small vessel into the air. When she spun it around, Reyes saw her in the cockpit. She threw a shooing motion at her to encourage her towards the mechs. All the while, the sound of the collapsing palace cracked around them.

Reyes took off at a sprint, large chunks of stalt falling from the ceiling at random points as she closed down on the line of giant metal humanoids. Behind her, Sparks opened fire on the guards, driving them back and sending a shower of crystal spraying up from the ground.

Despite there being a line of available mechs, Reyes only had eyes for one. When she reached them, she ran straight for the largest of the lot. So tall its head nearly touched the hangar's ceiling, it stood open, steps leading down from its chest. The steep climb almost too much for her, her legs wobbled as she got to the top, strapped herself in, and started the bot.

Two button presses and she encased herself like a mummy in an oversized sarcophagus. Before Reyes had worked out how to use it, Sparks came through to her on the radio.

"Reyes, this place is going to collapse any minute now. We need to get the hell out of here." All the while, Sparks continued to lay down fire against Enigma's army, keeping them pinned in the doorway. "You ready to go?"

After several more button presses, Reyes smiled as the mech lifted into the air. Her favourite thing to fly in the entire galaxy. Although her smile quickly faded; too much had happened for it to last. "Ready when you are, Sparks."

A second or two more of shooting, Sparks then spun her ship around and boosted out of there.

Even through the mech suit, Reyes heard the creaking and groaning of a palace about to collapse. She followed Sparks out into the crystal landscape.

CHAPTER 49

Despite the destruction ripping through the palace beneath his feet, Seb still heard boosters. A second later, he saw a small vessel and a mech rising from out of the building. Several ships burst out after them, clearly trying to hunt them down rather than escape themselves.

Seb already knew who piloted both vessels, but he waited for the confirmation. Both the mech and the ship flew straight at him, skimming over the roof of the palace. The mech caught up to him first and spoke with Reyes' amplified voice. "We've stopped the transmission from getting out, but Enigma cut Bruke's leg off, and SA's dead. I'm so sorry, Seb. Take her down, and we'll get the hell off this planet."

It took for both Reyes' mech and Sparks' ship to fly past before the words truly sank in. Where Seb had been painfully aware of the cracking and popping structure beneath him, it suddenly vanished with his concern for his own safety. His attention back on the woman with the green eyes, he saw the serenity had left her. His fists clenched, he spoke through gritted teeth. "Who are you?"

"It doesn't matter who I am. It's what I stand for."

A bubbling rage boiling within him, Seb stepped close to the woman, another shudder running through the soles of his boots. "You stand for evil. Death, destruction, deceit. You might have fooled yourself into thinking you represent something good, but you don't fool me. *Nothing* good can come of all the lives lost because of you. The lives lost to brutal regimes that you've supported. The lives of the slaves devastated from being forced into a living hell, and the carnage you've let loose on the galaxy. Thousands, if not millions, are dead because of *you*!"

No more than a background noise, the ships that had followed Reyes and SA out of the palace soared overhead. Their engines wailed and their blasters pulsed as they laid down rapid fire against his two friends.

A loud crash to Seb's right broke his focus on the green-eyed woman. A large section of the palace had crumbled and fallen to the ground. It wouldn't be long before the entire structure went with it.

Seb looked out into the stalt desert and saw guards escaping the building in every direction. They were so far away they looked like ants.

One of the ships exploded above them, the grey cloud of smoke broken by Reyes flying her mech through it.

Seb turned back to the woman. Although tears filled his eyes, fire roared within him. "SA and Bruke? One dead, the other mutilated!" The sadness he felt when she'd tried to take him over must have been for his friends. For his love. Were it not for the grief derailing him, the green-eyed woman would have taken control of him.

As Seb stepped closer to the woman, the woman stepped back, cracks and pops of breaking stalt all around them. So what if he went down with it? As long as she did too. "Did you even know my mother?" Before she could answer, he said, "You got into my head, didn't you? You mined my weaknesses and used them against me. But I think what you said about me being a transmitter was right. You wanted to use me as a tool." Another splash of collapsing stalt as another section of the palace fell. "And now you have *nothing*, no transmitter in the palace, and you won't be using my mind."

The woman with the green eyes finally spoke, pressing her hands together as if praying. "It'll work. We can change the galaxy forever with this. We're so close to seeing it through."

When Seb didn't reply, she pointed at him, her finger shaking. "And if you don't, you'll have to live with the consequences. You'll have to live with things exactly as they are now."

A life without SA hardly seemed worth living anyway. "How do you know it would work to use me as a transmitter? What evidence do you have that I could even do it?"

"It's what SA's been doing to communicate to everyone."

"What?"

"Ask her." A wicked smile streaked the woman's face as she covered her mouth, pretending to be shocked. "Oh, that's right, you *can't*."

The raging furnace burning within Seb spilled over. Lava ran through his veins, and he clenched his steel-lined fists. The ferocity of the wind grew and swirled around him as if reacting to his increasing power. Another ship exploded above them, a large flaming engine falling from it and shattering through another part of the palace.

Without knowing how he did it, Seb reached out with a shaking hand and held the green-eyed woman in place. He had total control, and the stretch of her wide eyes showed she knew it. Although he remained on the spot, his mind rushed forwards, directly into hers.

So dark in her head it made Seb's skin crawl. Veiled in shadow, he couldn't see anything. Then he turned a mental spotlight on, and he saw her truth. He saw the lies she'd told him. Although still in her mind, he spoke aloud, a vague awareness of everything falling apart around him. "You're not my aunt at all. You never knew my mum and dad. You pulled that out of my head. You lied about *everything*." As he delved deeper into her mind, he said, "SA was using me to project her telepathy, but she didn't know that. You wanted me to think she was manipulating me."

The power surging through Seb swelled as a pulse, a deep thrum of energy. And he had more to give ... lots more. He reached out to every slave in the galaxy. He felt their insanity, their sadness. He felt their fear and their fury. He pulled it all into him, relieving them of their suffering and the desire to inflict it on others. Every being screamed through his mind— a hive of chaos, thousands of voices deep.

Seb gathered it as a swirling mass. He shook as if he'd burst. Then he fixed on the woman in front of him, the woman in white with the green eyes. She looked weak now. He loosed a scream that shook the heavens before sending every shred of torment he'd pulled into himself at her.

Confusion in her green eyes, they spread wide with panic before she opened her mouth in a silent scream. Too much to even vocalise, she couldn't escape the feeling of what she'd been responsible for. Every shred of pain she'd inflicted was forced into her. Three more ships blew up in the sky above him while he held the woman, making her live the torment of what she'd created. The palace shook again, another section of it falling in on itself.

When Seb let go of the green-eyed woman, he watched

her clamp her hands to the sides of her head as if she could contain the burden. She then dropped them and released a throat-tearing scream before running at a flat-out sprint towards the edge of the palace's roof. A second later, she vanished over it.

When Seb caught up and looked down, he saw her broken body on the stalt below. Blood pooled beneath her head, growing ever wider as a crimson halo. Despite the power of his ancestors surging through him, giving him the ability to rip her limb from limb—even with the distance between them—he opted to kick a loose piece of stalt from the roof instead.

He watched as it sailed down and hit the now dead woman in the face.

CHAPTER 50

It took for the palace to shake beneath Seb's feet again to snap his attention away from the dead woman below. The wind continued unrelenting while a dogfight raged overhead. Reyes and Sparks flew through the air, lighting it up with the explosions of Enigma's ships. One after the other, their enemy fell, bursting into flames, smoke rising while their vessels dropped from the sky and shattered what remained of the stalt structure below.

But for every one they took down, two more appeared from the side of the palace. Like wasps leaving a nest, a steady stream of Enigma's ships burst into the sky, the air getting more treacherous for his two friends. Although his mind wanted to go to SA, Seb fought to focus on the problem at hand. He'd have time to grieve when he got out of there.

The same fire burning inside him, Seb moved his words into Sparks' head. *I need you to be ready to pick me up.*

Seb? Her ship wobbled as she flew. *How are you doing this? Is SA alive?*

The words rocked him, and it took a second to regain his

composure. *No, she's not. I can do it now too.* More cracks ran through the soles of his boots. *I need you to come down and get me out of here.*

What about Enigma's ships? I can't leave the battle.

Just do it, Sparks. Trust me.

Another shuddering *snap* where he stood. He didn't have long before it fell. As he watched Sparks close in—everything in slow motion—he saw half the palace collapse in one rushing avalanche of glittering crystal. Glass dust kicked up into the sky before being dispersed by the strong wind. Thankfully it blew away from him.

Sparks pulled up next to Seb a moment later. She hovered and opened the back door. Before he entered the vessel, he drew on the boiling fury within him. It charged like a plasma cannon, humming through his body before he yelled and thrust his arms out in front of him.

At least twenty Enigma ships now in the sky, they all simultaneously burst into flames. They fell as one, hitting the palace like a meteor shower.

The building shuddered again like an old beast ready to give up the ghost.

As Seb stepped onto Sparks' ship, he saw the small Thrystian staring at him with her mouth open. His attention quickly fell on the delirious Bruke, and his hands buzzed. While sliding to his knees next to his friend, he felt the ship still hadn't moved. "Get us out of here, now! And tell Reyes to retreat. We're going back to Aloo."

Sparks lifted the ship just as the vast stalt structure collapsed. The deafening rush of broken glass released an upward draft that sent them weaving from side to side. After a few seconds of riding it out, Sparks levelled the vessel again. She shot away while speaking to Reyes on the radio. "Come on, we're going back to Aloo."

His hands still on Bruke, Seb thought of SA buried within the building. No way could they retrieve her body from that; when the time came, they'd have to bury her memory in an empty casket.

CHAPTER 51

On their flight back to Aloo, Seb managed to stabilise Bruke. Not only did he offer him relief through the warmth he transmitted from his hands, but he managed to get into his friend's head and help switch off his pain receptors. He didn't know how he did it, but intuition guided him. The confrontation with the lady in white had unlocked in him a power he didn't know he had. The power of his ancestors. Maybe with the right guidance and intention, he could shift planets and move moons. But what did it matter? The thing that mattered most to him had been blown up and buried in tons of stalt.

As they touched down on the deck on top of the Shadow Order's base—the metal bottom of their ship crunching against the metal surface they landed on—Seb looked out of the window to see Reyes waiting. She'd left the mech with its back to them, the huge sentry standing strong and resolute as it looked out over the sea.

When Sparks opened the door, the strong rush of salty wind almost smelled like home. A sure sign he needed to move on.

Before Seb stepped outside, Reyes wheeled a gurney over to them. Together they lifted the heavy Bruke onto it.

They'd gone down in the elevator many times before. They'd existed in the post-battle exhaustion together plenty of times too. They'd even shared the loss of Gurt. Now they shared the loss of SA.

The elevator stopped and the doors opened, the sound of the mechanism almost deafening because of their silence.

Sparks said it first. "What the hell's happened here?"

Seb and Reyes pushed Bruke out into the wrecked gunmetal grey corridor. Lights blinked as if about to short out, ceiling panels hung down, and dents lined the walls on either side.

As much as Seb tried to feel for danger, he couldn't sense any. Instead he called out, "Hello?"

Almost like he'd been waiting for them, Moses walked around the corner. His wide jaw hung loose as he looked at the four of them. Dark and tear-filled eyes, they lingered on Bruke before turning to Seb. "I'm so, so sorry."

Whatever Seb had held on to until that moment abandoned him; safe at last, his legs buckled. He hit the ground hard, and as he blacked out, he heard Moses order another being to take Bruke away for surgery.

CHAPTER 52

Seb woke to find Moses leaning over and staring concern down on him. Pains in every muscle in his body, lethargy sat as a deep stagnation within them. A fur-lined tongue, a taste in his mouth like something had died in it, he tried to speak, gave up, and made a long groaning noise instead.

"You're a hero, Seb Zodo," Moses said. "You broke Enigma's hold on the slaves. You liberated them."

Disorientated from his sleep, Seb sat up too quickly. His world spun and nausea clamped his stomach tight. He held his pounding head and groaned again. "I feel like I'm going to die. How long have I been out for?"

"Two days."

"*Two days?*" Childish hope, no more, yet he still asked it. "Anything from SA?"

Moses spoke with a sigh, reaching across and holding Seb's hand. "SA's dead. She didn't get out of the palace. Anything crushed in that mess ... well ..."

As much as he knew he should eat, when Moses offered him bread, Seb's stomach sank. It felt like he'd never eat again, his grief a tumour in his gut.

Although in his room, it looked very different from how Seb had left it. Whatever had happened in the corridor had also passed through here. The walls were dented, and the ceiling tiles hung down. "What's happened to this place?"

"When the spaceport got too dangerous, Buster and Owsk had nowhere else to bring the slaves and contain them, so we used the base. They did quite a number on it. Thankfully you stopped them when you did; otherwise it would be beyond repair."

"Where are the slaves now?"

"Aloo."

"The spaceport?"

"Not a spaceport anymore; the ex-slaves need a home."

"What about your money earner here?"

"I think it's about time I earned money a different way." In the silence that followed, Moses wrung his hands and spoke to the floor. "We've been waiting for you to recover so we can have SA's funeral."

It felt like falling without end. Tense, his stomach doing backflips, and a lump of sadness wedged as a rock in his throat, Seb let out the longest exhale. As much as he didn't want a funeral for SA, he needed to be there, and avoiding it wouldn't change anything. Then he remembered what had happened to his friend. "How's Bruke?"

"Minus his left leg, but he's on the mend."

"Good. You can give him a new one?"

Moses nodded before he stood up and held a hand down to Seb. "Are you ready?"

"I'm not sure I'll ever be."

"Come on, Seb." Moses put his arm around him once he'd gotten to his feet. "We're right beside you."

CHAPTER 53

They stood on the landing platform at the top of the Shadow Order's base. The mech Reyes had flown in a few days previously remained on guard, watching the horizon. An empty box in front of them, the others had all said something. All heartfelt. All a reminder of exactly what Seb had lost.

With a look to either side of him, Seb took in his friends. Moses, Bruke, and Sparks on one side. Reyes, Owsk, and Buster on the other. Sparks reached up and wrapped one of her long hands around his. At first it triggered more tears. He'd given up wiping them, the cold saline spray stinging where his grief dampened his skin.

Then Seb let go of her and stepped forward. For a few seconds, he looked out to sea and watched the rise and fall of the waves. For the first time since he'd had his metal fists, he felt no panic. The fear of death didn't have the same hold on him. Death was nothing compared to his sense of loss. Death would be a relief. He finally looked down at the box and spoke. "What can I say? How can I verbalise the chasm of a hole that's been torn into my being? She was the strongest and most beautiful woman I've ever known. The only woman who's lived up to the memory of my mum. A heart of gold. Selfless."

For a moment he lost himself, another surge of tears streaming down his face. After wiping his nose, he continued, "Listen to me. The same bullshit everyone says at funerals. Like a few words can help with the pain. What's the point? It hurts. That's what I want to say. It hurts like hell, and I know this pain will *never* ease. Ever. In fact, it feels like it will get worse with time. That it will spread like a black hole, pulling all of me into it until I have nothing left. Besides, nothing I can say in these few short minutes can come close to summarising the woman I love and her many nuances. If I tried to write a book about what she meant to me and how wonderful she was, it would never end."

Although he could say more, he wouldn't ever know when to stop. After a look at the grief-distorted faces of his friends, he turned back to the coffin and shifted it to the edge of the platform. He then lifted one end, tilting it into the choppy water, the waves shifting it in his hands as the sea grabbed it, ready to pull it in. Then he let go and watched it sink. For a moment he nearly followed it. "Goodbye, my love."

His friends on either side of him—Bruke on crutches because he hadn't yet had an artificial leg fitted—they all watched the symbol of their friend vanish.

"She spoke," Reyes then said.

Rocked by the wind, Seb looked at the Hispanic marine. "Spoke?"

While biting her bottom lip, tears clinging to her cheeks against the blustery onslaught, Reyes nodded.

"What did she say?"

"That she loves you."

The sound came out of Seb as a tormented baseline issued from his diaphragm. His legs went again, but Moses caught him before he fell. He looked at Reyes. "How ... how did she sound?"

It took Reyes several attempts to pull her features under control enough to get her words out. She finally said, "Celestial."

CHAPTER 54

Just hours after SA's funeral, Moses told Seb he needed to go to Danu. He also told him he always had a home and place with the Shadow Order, but he'd fulfilled his obligation to them. He'd never want for anything because a steady stream of credits would go into his bank for the rest of his days.

Reyes and Sparks had decided to remain with Buster and Owsk. The Shadow Order would always have a purpose in the galaxy, and they weren't done fighting, in spite of everything. Bruke travelled with Seb to Danu.

When they stepped off the ship into the blustery and busy Danu spaceport, Seb saw two police officers look over at him. Other than Logan, he'd never seen eye to eye with Danu's law enforcement. Every instinct told him to walk the other way, but it wouldn't do them any good. Besides, Bruke only had one leg. They weren't exactly set up for a quick getaway. He'd not had time to get an artificial one fitted, so he'd chosen to travel with crutches to keep Seb company.

"Seb Zodo?" one of the officers said as they walked over to him.

Seb stared at both of them.

"We need you to come with us."

Seb continued to stare.

"It's about Logan."

An already broken heart, he'd had more than he could take. But what could he do? Run away?

CHAPTER 55

It didn't take for Seb to see the hospital to know it was bad. The sombre tone the officers had spoken to him in had been a well-practiced one. The one they gave to parents when they knocked on the door in the middle of the night. The look that told you everything before the words did. The conservative hope they tried to offer, more to make it easier on them because they knew your life was about to crumble.

As they closed in on the private room, Seb said, "Is he dead?"

By way of reply, one of the officers opened the door to let Seb in. Bruke waited outside with them.

The long Frant's feet hung from the end of the just-too-small bed. A steady pip of a heart monitor, his chest moved up and down with his breaths. Although the pause between inhale and exhale lasted that little bit too long each time, he clearly still hung on.

As Seb sat down next to his dad's old partner, his hands tingled. He reached over and placed them on the Frant.

It filled Logan's chest with the swell of a fuller breath, and he opened his eyes. He tilted his head to one side and looked at Seb. At first, his stare sat glazed like he didn't recognise him. Then clarity lit a torch in them, and he spoke with a croak in his voice. "Seb, how are you, son?"

"Not you too," Seb said, fighting against the buckle running through his bottom lip. "I've had about all I can take."

"I'm done, Seb. My time has come. We can't cheat death. No one can. But don't be sad for me. I've done all I came here to do."

"Why didn't you tell me you were ill?"

"I knew what you had ahead of you. I didn't want you worrying about me." Logan then reached across and put a hand on Seb's face. "I knew I could hold on to say goodbye." A moment's pause. "And I've done the house up too."

"What? You stayed alive to tell me that?"

"Hey, don't underestimate what I've done. I managed to give the place a lick of paint and tidy it up a bit. I got rid of all the sand and dust. That was no mean feat."

"You've held on so we could make small talk about my dad's house? Are you going to tell me to put the dishwasher on when I get in too?"

Logan smiled a weak and crooked smile. He stroked Seb's cheek with his thumb. "No, I've not. Sorry. I'm not very good at this. You've met every challenge thrown at you, Seb Zodo. I know for a fact your dad would be brimming with pride were he here now. If you do nothing else in this life, know that you've done more than many would in ten lifetimes. Hold your head high. You're one of the galaxy's greats."

The buzz still in his hands as he rested them on Logan, Seb cried.

When Logan lifted Seb's touch away from him, he resisted.

"Let me go, son. Let me be at peace. I'm ready. Let this be a celebration of us knowing each other."

How could he plead with the man to stay? A selfish request just so he didn't have to feel any more pain. Almost as hard as pushing SA's empty coffin into the water, Seb stared at the creature for a second before pulling his healing touch away from him. He held his hand instead and nodded. "You go to heaven now. If anyone's earned it, it's you."

Seb watched Logan nod back at him before he released his last breath in a long and weary sigh. His mouth remained open mid-exhale. His skin dulled, the life draining from him. The tall Frant's hand slowly turned cold in his.

CHAPTER 56

"Shouldn't we go back to Aloo to get your leg sorted?" Seb said as he slowed down his approach towards the chapel.

Although he walked on crutches, Bruke still managed to nudge Seb forward with his shoulder. "My leg can wait. This can't."

The building stood as an intimidating sight. Looming large, it dwarfed everything around it, the spire pointing up into the sky. Still and silent, Seb's heart rate trebled to look at it. "What if we're the only two beings here?"

"Even more of a reason to go."

When they arrived at the double doors to enter the place, Bruke shuffled ahead of Seb and pulled one of them open for him.

Even before they'd stepped inside, Seb saw the tight press of beings in the chapel. Over half of them were dressed in the uniform of Danu's police force. The other half were beings he'd never seen before. A Frant in uniform stood at the front of the room, looking out over the two hundred or so beings present.

At first, just one of the creatures at the back turned around to see Seb. A few seconds later, many more did the same. They parted for him, letting him through and showing him his path to two empty seats at the front.

When Seb sat down, the Frant at the lectern smiled at him before looking out over the gathered crowd, his eyes radiant.

"I had a long speech planned for today," the Frant said. "It tried to cover all the things Logan was to all the different beings I knew would be here. A friend, a father figure, a protector, a servant ... He was many things to many beings. But as I stand here now before you, I want you all to take a moment to look around this chapel to see what I'm looking at. It says more than I ever could. You measure the worth of a being by their friends. No words can come close to this."

As Seb looked around the room at all of the beings there, he saw the same expression on every face. Sure, he saw plenty of tears, but he also saw beaming positivity despite their sadness. They glowed with the privilege of having had Logan in their life.

In spite of himself, when Seb looked at Bruke, he smiled too. Logan was right. Death didn't always have to be sad.

CHAPTER 57

Bruke put his leg operation off for even longer, remaining with Seb for a few days after Logan's funeral. He worried about leaving him on his own. The sentiment meant a lot to Seb, but truth be told, since Bruke had left that morning, he felt glad to simply sit in his dad's old chair in front of the open fire.

With everything that had gone on since he'd last been in Danu, he felt ready for a rest. Depression or exhaustion, he couldn't tell. Either way, he needed to give it time. As he eased back in his dad's comfy chair, the flickering fire hypnotising him, his eyes lost focus.

Then it hit him. Much like the visions the woman in white had put into Seb's mind, he saw her. Although this time, not his mum. SA.

The shock of the vision pulled Seb back into the front room in his dad's house. He couldn't see SA any more. She'd been wandering across the stalt desert on Varna, blind and lost. It couldn't be. She hadn't gotten out of the palace. Just wishful thinking, nothing more.

Seb's heart ached, and he focused on his breaths to try to

ease the lump in his throat. SA was dead. Whether he wanted to or not, he had to accept it.

The front door then rattled and opened. It snapped Seb from his spiralling thoughts. No doubt Bruke had forgotten something. He called out, "What have you left behind?"

But Bruke didn't reply.

The door closed gently, cutting off the sound of the fierce wind outside.

Hearing footsteps in the hallway, Seb pushed off against the chair's armrests and got to his feet.

As the steps drew closer, Seb's world slowed down and he clenched his fists. Surely Bruke would have spoken by now. While biting on his bottom lip, he walked to the living room's door, held his breath, and pulled it open.

Time stopped as they both stared at one another. Butterflies in his stomach, and his chest feeling like it could burst as his entire being swelled, Seb finally said, "SA?"

The brilliance of her bioluminescence shone with even more radiance than he remembered. She had cuts and bruises all over her face from where the palace must have fallen on her. They did nothing to mar her beauty. She smiled. "Hi."

The voice he'd always heard in his mind, but much richer ... fuller ... celestial. "You're talking!"

While scratching the top of her head as if shy in front of him, she looked at her feet. When she lifted her gaze again, her cheeks flushed as she said, "Is now a good time to start that life we planned?"

THE END.

Thank you for reading Prophecy - Book Seven of The Shadow Order.

Want more of the Shadow Order? Reyes becomes an important member of the Shadow Order from book five onwards. Get to know her in 120-Seconds: A Shadow Order Story - Information available at www.michaelrobertson.co.uk

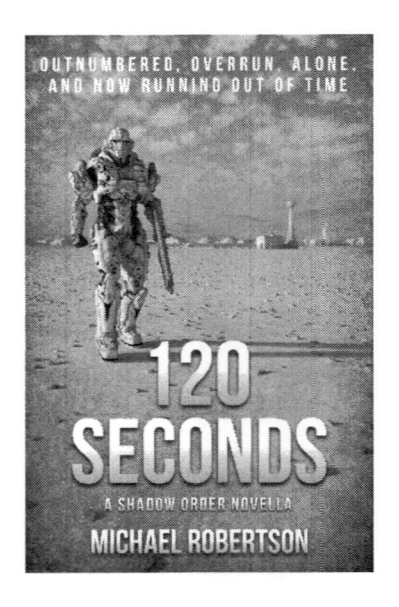

Support the Author

DEAR READER, AS AN INDEPENDENT AUTHOR I DON'T HAVE the resources of a huge publisher. If you like my work and would like to see more from me in the future, there are two things you can do to help: leaving a review, and a word-of-mouth referral.

RELEASING A BOOK TAKES MANY HOURS AND HUNDREDS OF dollars. I love to write, and would love to continue to do so. All I ask is that you leave an Amazon review. It shows other readers that you've enjoyed the book and will encourage them to give it a try too. The review can be just one sentence, or as long as you like.

∽

IF YOU'D LIKE TO BE NOTIFIED OF ALL MY NEW RELEASES AND special offers, you can sign up to my spam-free mailing list at www.michaelrobertson.co.uk

∽

If you've enjoyed The Shadow Order, you may also enjoy my post-apocalyptic series - The Alpha Plague - Book 1

<u>**The Alpha Plague - Available Now**</u>
<u>**Go to www.michaelrobertson.co.uk**</u>

A Post-Apocalyptic Action Thriller
THE
ALPHA
PLAGUE
MICHAEL ROBERTSON

MASKED - A PSYCHOLOGICAL HORROR

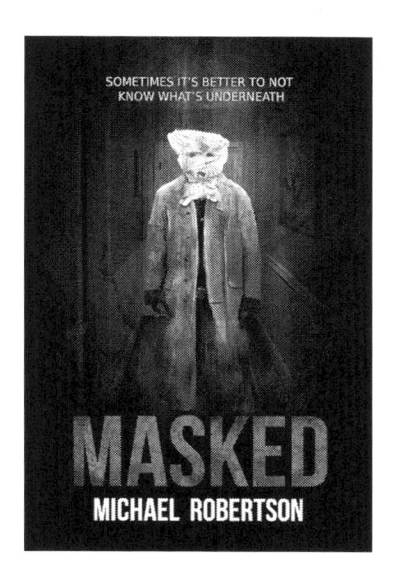

SOMETIMES IT'S BETTER TO NOT KNOW WHAT'S UNDERNEATH ...

Jacob Davies is an alcoholic who's been sober for twenty years. When he watches his dad lose his battle against pancreatic cancer it sends his life into chaos and the cravings return stronger than ever. Lost in his grief, he starts to see visions of a masked man that no one else can see. A man who knows things Jacob is yet to find out. A man who has answers to questions Jacob didn't realise he had.

Lucy, Jacob's wife, stood by him the first time he fell into alcoholism. As he starts to drink again, she makes it perfectly clear she won't do it a second time. Not now they have two teenage children to protect.

The visions and Jacob's grief send him on a journey that leads him to the brink of losing both his family and sanity. As he tries to hold everything together, maybe his only way out is to understand why he's seeing the masked figure ...

... Although maybe it will make everything a hell of a lot worse.

Masked is a psychological horror about grief, addiction, and deceit.

For more information, go to www.michaelrobertson.co.uk

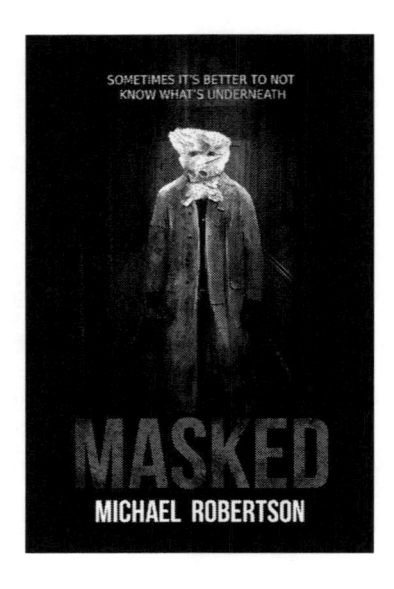

Praise for Masked

5 Stars *****

I was not prepared for this novel. It brought out so many mixed emotions. Michael had done it again with a great read.

5 Stars *****

This one is as good as any horror written by King or Koontz.

5 Stars *****

This novel blew my mind away!

ABOUT THE AUTHOR

Like most children born in the seventies, Michael grew up with Star Wars in his life. An obsessive watcher of the films, and an avid reader from an early age, he found himself taken over with stories whenever he let his mind wander.

Those stories had to come out.

He hopes you enjoy reading his books as much as he does writing them.

Michael loves to travel when he can. He has a young family, who are his world, and when he's not reading, he enjoys walking so he can dream up more stories.

Contact
www.michaelrobertson.co.uk
subscribers@michaelrobertson.co.uk

ALSO BY MICHAEL ROBERTSON

Masked - A Psychological Horror

∽

The Shadow Order
The First Mission - Book Two of The Shadow Order
The Crimson War - Book Three of The Shadow Order
Eradication - Book Four of The Shadow Order
Fugitive - Book Five of The Shadow Order
Enigma - Book Six of The Shadow Order
Prophecy - Book Seven of The Shadow Order
120-Seconds: A Shadow Order Story

∽

The Alpha Plague: A Post-Apocalyptic Action Thriller
The Alpha Plague 2
The Alpha Plague 3
The Alpha Plague 4
The Alpha Plague 5
The Alpha Plague 6
The Alpha Plague 7
The Alpha Plague 8

∽

Crash - A Dark Post-Apocalyptic Tale
Crash II: Highrise Hell
Crash III: There's No Place Like Home
Crash IV: Run Free
Crash V: The Final Showdown

∼

New Reality: Truth
New Reality 2: Justice
New Reality 3: Fear

Printed in Poland
by Amazon Fulfillment
Poland Sp. z o.o., Wrocław